It's witch-hunt time . . .

a time when men betray their friends and abandon their mistresses to escape the dread attentions of the House Committee on Un-American Activities.

For Howard Prince, who knows as little about HUAC as HUAC knows about him, the hour of destiny has struck.

But the fortunes of the great TV comedian Hecky Brown, blacklisted and ostracized, are going down, down, down. Now, if only Mr. Brown could recall the names of some of his old Commie friends, the Committee says, or do a bit of discreet spying on his friend Howard, perhaps his luck would improve. . . .

THE FRONT

The deliciously funny, achingly sad movie starring the inimitable Woody Allen as the fake screenwriter, Howard, and Zero Mostel as the brash, brilliant TV comic.

THE FRONT
is an original POCKET BOOK edition.

THE FRONT

Novelization by
Robert Alley

Screenplay by
Walter Bernstein

PUBLISHED BY POCKET BOOKS NEW YORK

THE FRONT

POCKET BOOK edition published October, 1976

This original POCKET BOOK edition is printed from brand-new
plates made from newly set, clear, easy-to-read type.
POCKET BOOK editions are published by
POCKET BOOKS,
a division of Simon & Schuster, Inc.,
A GULF+WESTERN COMPANY
630 Fifth Avenue,
New York, N.Y. 10020.
Trademarks registered in the United States
and other countries.

ISBN: 0-671-80739-0.

Printed in the U.S.A.

THE FRONT

One

Winter sunlight filled the canyons of Manhattan. Gray skyscrapers stood outlined against a clear blue sky that extended westward to the Hudson River and beyond. It was a fine March morning in 1953, a time of prosperity and some innocence. Gaudy billboards dominated Times Square, advertising everything from Camels to television sets that a wealthy nation was eager to buy. *South Pacific* had just entered its third year on Broadway. Christine Jorgensen's sex change was about to provide a favorite subject for conversation. And people all over America were busy dreaming up droodles.

But there was a dark cloud lurking on the horizon, reflected in the headlines that shuttled along the corridor of lights, high above Times Square:

NEW INQUIRY SEEKS REDS IN EDUCATION——MC-CARTHY AND NIXON SAY COMMIES MUST BE PURGED. . . . EX-ARMY SERGEANT FOUND GUILTY

OF BETRAYING SECRETS TO NORTH KOREANS. . . .
PRESIDENT EISENHOWER DENIES CLEMENCY IN
ROSENBERG SPY CASE. . . .

An atmosphere of suspicion and persecution had settled over the country, one that could not be dispelled by the best of weather.

One person affected by that atmosphere was Alfred Miller, a young television writer. As he emerged from the subway at Times Square, Alfred couldn't avoid seeing the headlines plastered across the front pages of the *Times* and the *Post*. The House Committee on Un-American Activities was conducting investigations of government employees and some ordinary citizens. They seemed remote—and implausible—to most Americans; but, for Alfred Miller, the investigations were very real.

Alfred was one of the best scriptwriters in the business. He was also an intellectual. He cared about the underprivileged people of the world, but he also enjoyed earning a thousand dollars for a script. In his crew-neck sweater, tweed jacket with square shoulders, pleated corduroy trousers, and cordovans, he seemed the epitome of success—handsome in an athletic way, with neatly trimmed hair and a strong, ready smile. Alfred had worked hard at writing and, until recently, had looked forward to a long and profitable career.

He entered the revolving door of the network's headquarters on Eighth Avenue. The receptionist in the lobby smiled at him, for Alfred was something of a celebrity. He nodded and stepped onto the elevator. He stepped off again on the eighth floor, and walked along the corridor toward the office of one of the network's many producers.

Alfred had been called in for a script conference.

He arrived, expecting to hear the usual congratulations, looking forward to being paid. No matter how much money he'd made from writing scripts, it always seemed to disappear: on his apartment, on books, on entertainment, and lately on doctors. During the last few months, Alfred had developed an ulcer.

On this day, the producer received him without the usual enthusiasm. He sat with his elbows propped on his desk on either side of a silver ashtray that was brimming with cigarette butts, holding Alfred's script. His full head of gray hair was smoothly combed, but he seemed tired, distracted.

"Sorry, Alfred," he said, "I can't use your stuff anymore."

Alfred felt the blood drain from his face.

"What's wrong with them?" he asked.

"Nothing. They're wonderful. You're a wonderful writer."

Alfred waited for him to explain, but the producer just tossed the script onto the desk. He shook his head, avoiding Alfred's eyes.

"It's a damned shame," the producer said.

The lights of the rehearsal studio were blinding. Alfred made his way carefully among the folding chairs, holding the script up to shield his eyes. He barely heard the voices of the actors, barely noticed the thick cables over which he had to step.

Another scriptwriter, a middle-aged man in a plaid, sleeveless sweater, sat alone in the back of the studio. Alfred took a seat next to him, talking in a low, urgent voice. The other writer listened, then wiped his face with a handkerchief.

"But we don't write the same way," he said.

"Who would know the difference?"

"Everybody knows the way I write." The writer shook his head, just as the producer had. "We'd just be making trouble for both of us."

During the next few days, Alfred approached every working writer he knew. He asked them to submit his script for production, with their own names on it. They all refused. Some were apologetic, some were curt. All of them were scared.

One writer, a personal friend of Alfred's, claimed he was not emotionally capable of helping.

"It's not me, Al," he protested. "It's my analyst. I'd like to help you, really. But he thinks, at this point in my therapy . . ."

"I understand," said Alfred. And he did understand. Helping him meant taking a big risk.

Later that night, at a movie in Times Square, hoping to forget the misfortune that had overtaken him, Alfred was surprised to see the box office surrounded by pickets, most of them wearing hats of American Legionnaires. They carried placards that read JOHN GARFIELD IS UN-AMERICAN and BOYCOTT COMMIE MOVIES, and they shouted at people who tried to buy tickets. Most of the potential customers turned and hurried away, embarrassed and obviously afraid.

Alfred pushed through the crowd, and bought his ticket. As he was about to enter the theater, one of the pickets grabbed his arm and began to shout about Commie sympathizers. Alfred looked down at the man's face, twisted with rage, his lips curled back to reveal stained teeth, the skin wrinkled about his tiny eyes, his Legionnaire's cap pulled tight over a hairless skull.

He shook the man off and entered the theater. There were not a dozen people in the audience, although the film had just been released and had received good reviews. Alfred sat in the darkness, determined to enjoy the film, but his heart was beating very fast. He kept hearing the screams of the Legionnaires and remembering the man's face so full of hate.

Two

The tavern in Alfred's old neighborhood resembled a thousand others in Brooklyn. A clock donated by the Rheingold supplier hung above bottles of Scotch, bourbon, and rye. Booths lined one wall, where hot pastrami sandwiches and breaded cutlets were served with the pitchers of beer. Things had not changed much at the Friendly Tavern since Alfred was eighteen years old.

A soap opera was playing on the television set above the bar when Alfred came in the next day. He had not been there in months, but now he was on a very special mission. Alfred needed the help of someone outside the broadcasting industry—someone he knew who was willing to take a risk, and who needed money.

His old friend, Howard Prince, worked in the Friendly Tavern as a cashier. He stood at the bar, doing card tricks for the amusement of the good-looking waitress, obviously enjoying his own showmanship.

Howard was short and slight, with comical, black-rimmed glasses and a fly-collar shirt buttoned at the throat. His dark, unruly hair fell low on his forehead, and there was a mischievous quality in his eyes. Although in his mid-thirties, Howard was still uncomplicated and boyish. Alfred had never been able to understand Howard's appeal to women.

He walked up behind him, and said, "Hello, Howard."

"Allie!" Howard's face lit up with surprise and pleasure. "Why didn't you tell me you were coming?"

"Just thought I'd drop by."

They shook hands.

"I was thinking about you the other night," Howard said. "I saw your show on TV." He jerked his thumb in the direction of the patrons at the bar. "What I had to do to get those clowns to turn off the ball game."

Alfred was pleased. But he wondered if that would be the last of his shows anyone would ever see.

"This is my friend, Alfred Miller," said Howard, introducing him to the waitress. "He's the big TV writer. And this is Margo, the big waitress."

Margo was big. Her breasts strained the buttonholes of her sheer blouse.

"Hi," Alfred said. He had other things on his mind. "Howard, I thought before the dinner rush . . . I thought we could take a walk, maybe play a little chess."

Howard was delighted. "Will you take care of the register, Margo?"

"Sure," she said, smiling affectionately.

"Unless you're too busy . . ." Alfred was still hesitant to involve him.

"For you?"

Howard slipped into his two-tone gabardine windbreaker with buttons on the cuffs and a leather tassel on the zipper. They headed out the door together.

"Hey, Howard," called the bartender. "What's the price on the Kid Gavilan–Carmen Basilio fight?"

Howard was not just the cashier in the Friendly Tavern. He was also the local bookie.

He paused to figure the odds, then said, "Eight to five—Gavilan."

The bartender chuckled. Howard was not the most successful bookmaker in the neighborhood.

"I'll take Basilio five times."

"You got it," Howard said cheerfully.

He and Alfred headed up the street, toward Flatbush Avenue, and the little park on the corner where they had spent a lot of time together. Alfred tried to make conversation about Howard's favorite subject, after girls: sports.

"You think Brooklyn again? Or the Cardinals?"

Howard held up two crossed fingers. "Better be Brooklyn. I'm loaded with Cardinals."

"The game is pitching . . ."

"Well," Howard interrupted, on second thought, "the Dodgers have got that Erskine, Branca and Preacher Roe. They could go all the way this year."

"They're a rough team, the Cards—lot of speed."

Howard liked to argue. "What good's speed, if you can't get on base?"

It felt like old times.

They crossed Flatbush Avenue and sat down at the chess table in the park. The brick wall of an adjacent building trapped the sunlight, warm and relaxing, reminding them that spring would soon arrive.

Howard took the chess pieces from the pocket of his windbreaker, and set them up on the board. He held the two queens behind him. Alfred picked the white queen, and opened the game with the king's pawn. But he had trouble concentrating.

After a particularly long pause, Howard said gently, "Your move."

Alfred reached for his knight, then dropped his hand. It was no use going on.

"Howard," he said, "I can't work."

Howard was sympathetic, as always. "Writer's block?"

Alfred shook his head.

"You're not sick?" Howard persisted.

"I'm blacklisted."

Howard didn't understand what that meant, although he wouldn't admit it.

"But you feel all right?"

"I feel terrible."

"But you're healthy. I mean, besides your ulcer."

Alfred pushed the chessmen aside. "They won't buy my scripts. I'm on a blacklist. You know what that means?"

Howard just grinned—proof that he didn't know.

"It's a list of names, Howard. The networks have them—the ad agencies, the movie studios. You're on that list, you're marked lousy. You don't work. So what difference does it make if I'm healthy?"

"It makes a difference." For Howard, life was simple—you took care of yourself. "What are you blacklisted for?"

"I'm a Communist sympathizer."

"But you always were."

Alfred sighed. "It's not so popular anymore."

Back in the 1930s, all the intellectuals had been sympathetic to Communism. Alfred was a student then and, like all students, he wanted a better world. Communism was not considered anti-American in those days. It was considered progressive. Now Alfred and many people like him were suffering for their earlier belief. They were accused by right-wing organizations of being dangerous to national security, a charge that was as ludicrous as it was untrue.

Howard was amazed at Alfred's naïveté. Alfred had always been like that, even when they attended P.S. 161 together.

"How many times did I tell you?" Howard said. "Take care of Number One. Now, who can you sue?"

"Nobody. Nobody admits there's a blacklist. They just say your script's not good enough. Or that you're not right for the assignment."

"Then pay somebody off."

"This is not like making book, Howard." Alfred was getting exasperated.

"This is still America. There's always somebody you can pay off."

Alfred wished there *was* someone he could pay off, but his enemies were unseen and very powerful. They were modern-day vigilantes, beyond appeal, and they could influence the top executives of the biggest corporations. The vigilantes all sounded like Senator Joe McCarthy, the leader of the anti-Communists in Congress. *The enemies of the free world,* they said, had to be *ferreted out* because they were supposedly protected by *Commie-crats,* guilty of *coddling* and being *soft* on these *fellow travelers* who were *security risks.* . . .

"Isn't there someone you can lean on?" Howard asked.

Unfortunately, there wasn't anyone. Respect for the blacklist went to the top of the networks' management.

"I know some people," Howard said. "They're not

exactly *people,* but for fifty dollars they'll break a few legs, and you're not bothered anymore."

"That's not what I need."

"You need money?" Howard never had money, but he always had advice about it. "I happen to know a stock, believe it or not, which is low right now, but it's going through the roof."

Howard always had a stock.

"I need another name," Alfred said.

"Yeah, I can see that. Another name . . ." He thought for a moment. "Rappaport! Alfred Rappaport." Howard snapped his fingers. *"Arnold* Rappaport!"

"Pseudonyms won't work. They know blacklisted writers are using different names. They require a real person."

"Oh." Then Howard understood what Alfred was driving at. "Oh, of course!"

"Someone they can believe," Alfred added, "and I can trust."

"Naturally."

Howard Prince would become Alfred Miller. Or the other way around. That was no problem.

Alfred said, "I wouldn't ask if . . ."

"Who else would you ask? I'd be insulted."

"No one else would know, only you and me."

"When do we start?" Howard asked.

"Hold your horses. First find out what you're getting into."

"You want to use my name on your scripts, right?"

"It's not that simple."

"Life is complex," Howard said, "if you make it complex."

Alfred took a deep breath. His ulcer was giving him

hell; he fished a bottle of antacid tablets out of his pocket and popped two into his mouth.

"Howard," he said, speaking slowly, "in all friendship, you have a slight tendency to be full of shit." Howard was his only chance of survival now, and they both had to be careful. "Now, listen to me. Remember that show I wrote for in radio? 'Grand Central,' remember? Stories about the city."

Howard nodded. "I listened every week."

"Well, they're turning it into a TV series."

"Smart." Howard already felt like an insider.

"I was supposed to write for that series," Alfred said. "Now I can't."

"Now you can."

"That's only the first part," Alfred cautioned. "I write a script and send it in under your name. They buy the script . . ."

"Perfect." Howard was getting excited.

". . . and then they'll want to meet the writer."

"So?"

"You'll have to meet them. Really be the writer."

"So I'll be the writer." Howard saw that Alfred was doubtful. "I can do it. What's the big deal? And I want to do it. You're in trouble, and I'm your friend. What's a friend for?"

Alfred felt guilty. "These days you can get in trouble being a friend."

But Howard wasn't worried. "Life is a risk," he said.

Alfred wished Howard would take the proposal more seriously.

"I think you need an egg cream," Howard suggested. "For your stomach."

"Forget the egg cream." Alfred wondered if Howard could even pass himself off as an author of tic-tac-toe

—he'd never seen Howard read anything other than a racing form.

"I want to pay you for this, Howard."

"What do you mean, pay? What is that? A friend takes money?"

Alfred was firm. "Ten percent for each script. No arguments, now. You're always in hock; you can use the money. And I'd be paying that much to an agent anyway."

Howard hadn't considered that. "Ten percent?"

"Off the top."

"How much do you get for a script?"

"A name writer," Alfred said, "for a half-hour show —seven-fifty, maybe a thousand."

Howard's eyes grew wide. For once he was speechless.

"Less for an unknown," Alfred quickly added. "It depends on the show."

But Howard was already spending the money in his head.

"Go home and write," he urged Alfred. "Your troubles are over!"

Three

The Fulton Street market was jammed with housewives pulling shopping carts, delivery boys on bicycles, men in long white aprons pushing trolleys loaded with fresh Florida fruit, vegetables from the truck farms in Jersey, fish from the Brooklyn docks. The air was full of the cries of the stall owners as they hawked their produce, and the rumble of traffic from the parkway.

Howard made his way jauntily among the stalls, keeping an eye out for pretty girls. Soon the girls would all be wearing spring fashions—thin blouses, low-cut dresses. Howard felt good, although he had things to worry about.

Danny, the fruit seller, waited beside his stall, in the shadow of the awning. His watch cap was pulled down to the bridge of his nose. The strings of the apron barely spanned his stomach, and his forearms were like hams, but covered with hair.

Danny greeted Howard without speaking. That was

a bad sign, and Howard quickly explained why he couldn't pay Danny the money he owed him—yet.

"What are you pulling here?" Danny asked in a low, guttural voice. "You owe me for three winners already. What am I, some kind of charity?"

He began to roughly rearrange the apples on his stand.

"Don't get excited," Howard said. "Your money's coming."

"You book bets, you lose, you pay off." Danny was upset. Howard had never taken this long to pay off.

"What's the matter, don't you trust me?" Howard tried to appear insulted. "Your money's on the way."

"I don't want to get mad on you, Howard. We been doing business a long time." He balled up a massive fist. "Don't get me mad on you!"

Howard promised he wouldn't. Danny knew the same people Howard knew—the ones who broke legs for fifty dollars. Danny knew them better than Howard did.

Howard said good-bye, and headed for downtown Brooklyn. It was time to pay a visit to his brother, Meyer.

Meyer Prince owned a wholesale-furrier's outlet. It was a thriving business—half sweatshop, half showroom—full of cutters, buyers, and occasional pretty models wrapped in mink, fox, and sable. Meyer didn't deal in imitation furs; he didn't need to. The shop smelled of success.

Howard enjoyed dropping by, to borrow money and look at the models. He liked to watch them strut and twirl in front of the jaded retailers from the city. But he didn't like the lectures his older brother always gave him.

Meyer received Howard in his private office. A

plate-glass window in the wall offered a view of the showroom; Meyer watched the action on the floor while Howard made his request. The diamond on Meyer's pinkie rose and fell in irritation. He was overweight, with thinning black hair, but his double-breasted suit was well tailored in sharp contrast to Howard's worn windbreaker.

"I don't understand you," he said finally. That was no surprise. Few people understood Howard. "What do you do with your salary, flush it down the toilet?"

"I had a tip on a stock," Howard said. Meyer didn't know his brother was a bookie. "It looked good, so I plunged."

Meyer was scornful. "Where do you come to stocks?"

Howard shrugged. He had caught the eye of a lithe brunette displaying the charms of a leopard-skin coat on the showroom floor.

"Why don't you ask me?" Meyer said, oblivious of Howard's flirtation. "I'm familiar with the market. Ask me before you flush your salary down the toilet."

"Next time I'll ask you," Howard promised.

Meyer leaned back in his leather swivel chair, and pressed his fingertips together. Meyer was married and a father—he was responsible. That was a word he used a lot, especially when he was lecturing his brother.

"Howard," he moaned, closing his eyes. "Howard, what's going to be with you? Momma and Poppa would turn in their graves."

"I haven't found myself yet." It was Howard's favorite line. "But it's all going to change. You'll see."

"You were always the smart one, Howard. Did I get the lessons?" Meyer had championed over adversity. That was another word he used a lot. "You could have gone to college. Instead, you're a bum."

Howard didn't protest. He knew he wasn't a bum, and he was going to prove it—with Alfred's help. But first he had to pay off Danny and the rest of the bettors he owed.

Meyer flopped a heavy checkbook on the desk. His gold ball-point pen hung in the air.

"How much this time?" he asked.

Howard decided to up the ante. "Six hundred."

"You said four on the phone."

"Four gets me even. Then I'm blank."

Meyer just stared at him.

"But I'm keeping strict accounts," Howard added.

"You said four; you get four."

Meyer wrote the check, ripped it out of the book, and tossed it across the desk. Howard caught it before it settled.

"Enough is enough," Meyer said. "I'm at the end of my rope, Howard. I got a business. You know what it costs to feed one lousy mink?"

Howard shook his head. How much could a mink eat?

"You know what a cutter gets today?"

Howard didn't know the answer to that one either. Business bored him.

"Thanks for the money, Meyer."

"At least if you were realizing your potential," Meyer went on, "I'd say fine, that's an investment."

"I'm working on it."

"At that cockamamie job you got?" Meyer laughed in disgust. "You call that a job? With a head like yours?"

"You're going to be surprised, Meyer." Howard couldn't wait to become a writer now.

"I'm serious," Meyer lectured. "The well is running dry. Sink, or swim."

He sounded like he meant it.

"Give my regards home," Howard said.

Going out, he didn't even glance at the brunette.

Howard's apartment was dark and cramped. He kept the shades drawn because he often preferred not to be at home to callers. A rolltop desk dominated the living room. It was covered with racing forms, scratch sheets, note pads, old newspapers, a well-used telephone, and a gooseneck lamp. The inside of the lampshade had been lined with tinfoil, to cast a better light on his failing business.

A studio couch sat at an angle, next to the window. It served as his bed. The tiny kitchenette cluttered with dirty dishes was rarely used for anything other than making coffee. The only possessions Howard valued hung on the walls of the apartment. These were photographs of girls—girls in bathing suits, in bobby socks, girls on the quay in Brooklyn Heights, riding on the Staten Island ferry, girls dancing with Howard at old high-school proms, girls sitting on Howard's lap, laughing with him, kissing him.

He sat at the rolltop desk in his shirt-sleeves, figuring the losses of his recent bookmaking. The four hundred dollars Meyer had loaned him was disappearing in a snap.

The telephone rang. Howard picked up the receiver as if it was alive and dangerous. He recognized the heavy breathing: Danny.

"Listen," Howard said, "I got hit very hard last week. The long shots were coming in like relatives."

Danny had always thought that was a funny line. But this time he didn't laugh. He wanted to know when Howard would pay him.

"I told you, soon. . . . Soon is soon. . . . Tomorrow, the day after . . ."

Howard liked to keep it casual. But Danny began to shout.

"What are you mad about?" Howard asked. "It's a promise. Trust me."

He hung up. The phone rang again almost immediately, and this time Howard answered in a badly disguised voice.

"Loew's Sheridan."

A girl asked to speak to Howard Prince.

"Who?" Howard had to be careful. She might be the wife of a creditor.

The girl repeated his name.

"Who wants him?"

"Florence Barrett."

Florence Barrett's voice was warm, precise, attractive. Howard tried to match it with a face.

"What do you look like?" he asked.

She hesitated, then said, "I'm assistant to Mr. Sussman, the television producer."

"Oh, yeah." Sussman was the producer to whom Howard had sent Alfred's new script—with Howard's name on it.

"Is this Howard Prince?" Florence Barrett asked.

"Yeah, I'm Howard Prince." And Howard added, "The writer."

"I enjoyed your script very much."

"You did?" Howard wished he had read the stuff before sending it in. "Well, I'm glad."

"We were wondering if you could drop by the studios. Mr. Sussman and I would like to meet you."

"Oh, sure." Howard wanted to meet her, too. "When?"

"Is tomorrow afternoon all right? If you write in the afternoons . . ."

"No, afternoons are fine." Were writers supposed to write in the afternoons? "I use the nights to write," he said, just in case. "Not so much noise, you know."

"Well, see you tomorrow, then."

"Great. See you."

"Bye." Florence Barrett sounded very sophisticated.

"Ciao," Howard said, hoping it made him sound cosmopolitan.

Four

The studio was crowded when Howard arrived the following afternoon. Hot lights beamed down on the set, where a group of actors stood rehearsing their lines. Men wearing earphones pushed large cameras around on rubber wheels. Thick cables snaked across the concrete floor; the script girl stepped over them as she ran beween the actors and the director, who sat behind the soundproof glass partition. His voice echoed over the loudspeakers.

Monitors on the floor showed the set in microcosm. When there was a pause in rehearsals, these same monitors were tuned into whatever was currently being broadcast—a hearing before the Senate Investigating Subcommittee, Senator Joseph McCarthy's dark, heavy jowls dominating the screens, as he jabbed the air with a blunt forefinger. The studio seemed far removed from the real world, but McCarthy's histrionics over the latest batch of Communist sympathizers served as a grim reminder of what was going on outside.

Howard stood by the soundproof door, watching the activity. He wore a soft knit tie and a wool jacket with padded shoulders. His shoes were shined. He was ready to be a writer.

He stopped a passing technician and asked for Florence Barrett. The man looked Howard over, trying to place him, then pointed to a couple standing near the set.

"The one with the hair," he said and walked on.

Florence Barrett was more attractive than Howard had imagined. And—what luck!—she wasn't taller than he was. She talked intently, shifting her weight from one foot to the other, her slim body unconsciously taking part in the conversation.

Actually, it looked more like an argument, with the man Florence Barrett was talking to losing. He was bald on the crown of his head, with thick black sideburns and heavy eyebrows. He seemed devoted to his own interests, yet curiously vulnerable.

Howard approached them, straightening his tie and buttoning his jacket. He stopped nearby, hands in his pockets, and waited to be recognized.

Florence Barrett was saying, "I won't tell him, Phil. You're the producer; do your own dirty work."

So that was Phil Sussman. Howard didn't know they were talking about an actor who was threatened with being blacklisted.

"All Hecky has to do is talk to the man," Sussman said.

"Why should he?" Florence was angry. "Who is this creep, anyway? So he worked for the FBI, where does he come off clearing anyone? Where does anyone come off?"

Sussman said, "It's for Hecky's own good."

"What's good about it? I'm against the whole rotten business."

"Who's in favor?" Sussman said, lowering his voice. "I'm against it, too."

"Then do something!"

Sussman was neither stupid nor evil, and at times he was even capable of generosity. But he didn't take chances.

"I don't run the network," he said.

Howard coughed discreetly. Sussman turned and stared at him.

"Can I help you?" he asked irritably.

"I'm Howard Prince."

"Who?"

But Florence recognized the name. "You're Howard Prince!"

She broke into a big smile, and offered her hand. Howard shook it.

"I'm Florence Barrett. I'm so glad you could come. Phil, this is Howard Prince, the writer. This is Phil Sussman, our producer."

Reluctantly, Howard let go of her hand and took Sussman's. "How do you do."

Sussman's irritation magically vanished. He pumped Howard's hand, revealing a capped smile and genuine enthusiasm.

"I'm sorry, I didn't connect the name," he said. "Listen, that's a hell of a script you wrote. Where have you been hiding?"

Howard shrugged modestly.

"We looked you up. No credits, no nothing. Just like that." Sussman snapped thick fingers. "Out of the blue!"

"I only took up writing a little while ago," Howard said.

"Well, it's a hell of a script. You got more?"

Howard raised his eyebrows. "Are you kidding?" Of course, he had more scripts. All Alfred had to do was write them.

Florence beckoned to two actors who came strolling over. One was tall and fair, and looked vaguely familiar. He was a character actor who had appeared in many television productions.

"Howard," Florence said, "this is Steve Parks, who plays our narrator."

Parks offered his hand.

"Marvelous script," he said coolly but with admiration.

"Thank you." Howard was still all modesty.

"And this is Hecky Brown . . ."

". . . who plays with himself," said the other actor, a short, pudgy figure with a face like a clown's, both funny and pathetic.

"Who plays the cabdriver," corrected Florence, while the others laughed.

Hecky covered his heart with both hands. His big, brown eyes filled with wonder. "Howie!" he gushed. "Howie Prince!" He threw his arms around Howard and kissed him wetly. "They let you out finally, darling!"

Howard knew he was being kidded, but Sussman took it straight.

"You know each other?" the producer asked.

"Never saw him before in my life," said Hecky. Then he slipped easily into another comic routine, that of an outraged woman. "Who is this man? Officer!"

They were all laughing now.

Florence gently disengaged Howard from Hecky's grip. "Excuse us. We have to talk."

"Seriously," Hecky said to Howard, "it's a first-rate script."

"Thank you."

Hecky and Parks ambled back to the set.

Howard felt warm all over. Things were going very well.

"We don't have too much time, Howard," Florence said. "That's why I asked you to come right away. We wanted to meet you, of course, but . . ."

"Your script's a little long," Sussman explained.

"Four-and-a-half minutes."

"I was going to suggest cutting the kitchen scene. I don't know how you feel about that."

"I think it's a mistake," Florence said quickly. "To me, the awkward scene is the one in the police station." She turned to Howard. "Don't you think?"

"Maybe." He put on his most serious expression. He hadn't expected to be asked about the script. "Maybe not."

That didn't seem to satisfy them.

"Depends on your definition of awkward," Howard added, trying to sound like he knew what the hell they were talking about.

"The police-station scene at least has some violence," Sussman said. He didn't want to sacrifice that.

But Florence was more interested in quality. "I'm not saying eliminate it. I just think it can be trimmed." She looked at Howard again. "What do you think?"

Howard opened his mouth, but nothing came out. He didn't know what to say, so he simply smiled.

"What?" said Sussman.

"Yes!" Howard was grasping at straws now.

"Yes, what?" asked Florence.

"Yes . . . I think there are many . . . many . . . a lot of facets here." That sounded professional enough.

"I don't want to just answer off the top of my head. It's not fair to you, not fair to the show."

Florence and Sussman seemed impressed with his sincerity.

"Look," Sussman said, "I know it's not fun to cut your script, but television is television. So you decide and you cut."

Howard pointed to himself. Surely, Sussman didn't mean that.

"I'm not the kind of producer who disembowels a writer's script." Sussman grasped Howard's arm. "I believe in the written word."

"Absolutely," said Howard.

"I need it tomorrow morning." Sussman shook Howard's hand again, smiling reassuringly. "But you be happy with it."

He walked away, leaving Howard and Florence alone together.

"I really liked your script a lot," she said.

"Thank you."

"Most of the stuff I read . . ." She paused, and said forcefully, "I mean, yours has *substance*. It's about people."

"Well, I feel if you're going to write about human beings, you might as well make them people." Howard laughed at his own joke. "You busy Sunday night?"

"Sunday?" Florence was surprised.

"That's my night off." Howard caught himself too late. "From writing," he added.

"I'm busy this Sunday."

"How about afternoons?"

A slight smile played across Florence's lips. She shook her head. "You work at night; I work during the day."

He wasn't going to be put off that easily.

"Don't you go out to lunch?"

"I usually have a sandwich sent in."

"That's not good for you," Howard said with authority. "I'll call you; we'll have lunch."

"All right." Florence was still smiling. "It was nice meeting you."

She turned and walked toward the set, where Sussman waited. Howard liked the way she moved, the way she looked, and the way she sounded. Florence Barrett had class, and she liked his script. He was going to enjoy being a writer.

He left the studio, heading for Alfred's apartment in Greenwich Village. He had time to drop off the script for a rewrite before reporting for work at the Friendly Tavern.

Florence and Sussman watched Howard leave.

"I had the pleasure of working with Bill Saroyan once," Sussman said wistfully. "This guy's got a lot of Bill's qualities—that shyness."

Florence wanted to laugh. Howard Prince was anything but shy.

Sussman turned to her, suddenly all business. "You won't tell Hecky?"

Their argument had been temporarily forgotten.

"Absolutely not," said Florence.

He sighed and walked toward Hecky to deliver the bad news in person.

Five

The Freedom Information Service occupied a suite of offices in a modern midtown skyscraper. The office walls were painted a military gray and hung with photographs of General Douglas MacArthur, President Eisenhower, Chiang Kai-shek, and J. Edgar Hoover. A dour-looking receptionist divided her time between answering the Service's telephone and addressing envelopes to important executives all over the city. These envelopes contained lists of persons the Service judged to be sympathetic to Communism, along with bills for the Service's investigations.

Hecky Brown was presenting himself to the receptionist, hat in hand. He'd been summoned by the Service's director, Francis X. Hennessy. Sussman had said the visit was just a formality, but Hecky couldn't get rid of the hollow feeling in the pit of his stomach. He knew a lot of actors who had been to see Hennessy.

Francis X. Hennessy sat waiting, his hands folded on the desk, crew-cut and unsmiling. A large American flag hung on the wall behind him, and his desk was piled with bound volumes of testimony before Congressional committees investigating subversion in the United States. Hennessy had intensely blue eyes and the expression of a man who believes that what he is doing is right. He stared at Hecky without speaking.

The telephone rang and Hecky jumped. He heard the receptionist say, "Freedom Information Service. . . . Who's calling? . . . One moment, please."

The intercom buzzed. Hennessy flipped the switch, still staring at Hecky.

"Mr. Hampton from the network," said the receptionist.

Hennessy picked up the telephone. He pointed to a hard wooden chair, indicating that Hecky should sit, and said, "Hennessy here."

Hecky's nervousness increased. Tom Hampton was an important person at the network.

"Yes, Tom," Hennessy, smiling thinly. "Yes, of course. First name Howard." He scribbled the name on a pad. "Got an address on him? Social Security number?" He carefully wrote the information down. "I'll check him right out. . . . No trouble at all, Tom. That's what you're paying me for. . . ." Hennessy's gaze settled on Hecky again. "Yes, as a matter of fact, he's here right now. I'm sure we'll work something out."

Hecky wasn't so sure. Why did Hennessy look at him like that? Why did an important man like Tom Hampton have to deal with Francis X. Hennessy?

"Call you as soon as I know anything about Prince," Hennessy said. ". . . . You, too, Tom. Carry on."

He hung up and studied the information he had just written down. The network's new scriptwriter would also have to be investigated.

"Sorry, Mr. Brown," Hennessy said at last.

"Hecky. Everyone calls me Hecky." He always talked too fast when he was nervous. "I'm a household name."

Hennessy didn't seem to hear. "I can't promise anything, you understand."

Hecky realized that the meeting was not a formality. He was in trouble.

"But if you simply tell me the truth," Hennessy added, "I might be able to help."

"I'll tell you the truth; I'll do anything."

Hecky knew what it meant to be blacklisted. People not only lost their jobs, but lost the respect of colleagues and friends. Their invitations were ignored. No one would play with their children. Hecky had heard that the son of a blacklisted actor was prevented from joining the Boy Scouts.

The thin smile returned to Hennessy's lips. "The question, Mr. Brown, is what have you *done?*"

"Nothing."

Hennessy's smile dissolved.

"I'm an actor," Hecky explained.

Again Hennessy didn't seem to hear. "Nothing?" he repeated.

Hecky knew he would have to admit something, confess, then apologize.

"Six years ago," he said, "I marched in a May Day parade."

Hennessy seemed to already know about that.

"I bought a subscription to *The Daily Worker,*" Hecky added. "But I never read it, not one word. From the mailbox right to the garbage can."

Hennessy was impassive. He began to inspect his fingernails.

"I was only trying to get laid," Hecky lamented.

"This girl, this Communist girl, she had an ass . . ."

Hecky shaped her ass in the air with his hands.

"I'm not interested in your sex life, Mr. Brown."

"Hecky." He tried to control his nervousness. "I'm just telling you, she was the reason."

Hennessy glanced down at a sheet of paper on his desk.

"Was she also the reason," he said, "that you signed a petition for Loyalist Spain?"

"Did I do that?" People used to sign any petition that came along. It was the thing to do.

"And Russian War Relief?" said Hennessy.

"We were on the same side, weren't we?"

Hennessy didn't answer.

"She was the reason," Hecky repeated. "Honest."

"Would you say, then, that you were duped?"

"Tell me what it means and I'll say it." Hecky was no intellectual. "You want it in writing? Tell me what to write."

"It has to come from you, Mr. Brown."

"Hecky," he said automatically."

"From your heart." Hennessy leaned toward him, across the desk. "It has no value otherwise."

"It'll come, don't worry." Hecky had begun to sweat. "I'm an actor. What do I know from politics?"

Hennessy returned to his fingernails.

"People all over the country write me letters," Hecky said. He thought maybe Hennessy wasn't aware of his popularity. "When this business happened, believe me, you could have knocked me over with a feather."

Hecky's obvious distress seemed to satisfy Hennessy. He nodded, as if some decision had been reached.

"Write me a letter, Mr. Brown. In your own words. How you were duped, how you feel about it now."

"I'm against it—a hundred percent."

But Hennessy wasn't finished. "Whomever else you remember in that parade, who asked you to sign those petitions."

Hecky knew that any names he provided would be added to the blacklist. But Hennessy had him over a barrel.

"Such a long time ago," Hecky said, rubbing his chin. "And I've got such a bad memory for names. Ask anybody, Mr. . . ." He pretended to forget Hennessy's name. "Mr. Morrison?"

Hennessy was not fooled.

"Try to remember," he urged Hecky, his blue eyes steady and unblinking. "Sincerity is the key, Mr. Brown. Anyone can make a mistake. The man who repents *sincerely* . . ."

"I repent," Hecky pleaded. "Sincerely."

"Write me the letter, Mr. Brown. I'll see what I can do."

Hecky was dismissed. He stood, waiting for Hennessy to say something more, but he was already bent over the papers on his desk.

Hecky walked to the door. Before going out, he said, "And I didn't even get laid."

Hennessy never looked up.

The first production of the new television series, "Grand Central," was scheduled for the following week. It was anxiously anticipated by Howard, Alfred, Florence, Sussman, Hecky, and even Meyer. They all had their own reasons for hoping it would be a success.

On the night of the broadcast, the studio atmosphere was tense. Sussman paced the control room, scanning the half-dozen television screens showing different angles of the set as the director sat by the levers, ready to call the shots. Florence stood silently in the back of the room, too nervous to sit. And Hecky, as he took his place before the cameras with the other actors, was wondering if this would be his last show.

Downtown in the Village, Alfred sat alone in his study, holding a glass of milk. He was unshaven and his ulcer was throbbing. The television screen provided the only light in the room, palely illuminating his typewriter and pages of a new script he had begun to write.

Across the East River, in Brooklyn, Meyer Prince hunched over a plate of steak and boiled potatoes. His television set was in the dining room, and he watched it as he ate. His wife sat with him. Neither of them had believed Howard when he said he wrote the script for the new show. They'd have to see it with their own eyes.

Twenty blocks away, in the Friendly Tavern, Howard stood beside the cash register. The television set over the bar was tuned in to "Grand Central." The bartender, the customers, Nat the owner, Margo, and the other waitress watched as the commercial faded, and the action began. For the first time Howard could remember, they were all quiet.

The half-hour passed quickly, effortlessly. When the show was over, everyone remained riveted, including Howard. He had no idea he was so good.

Finally, Margo turned to him, tears in her eyes. "Howard. Oh, Howard!"

The credits began to roll across the screen. When the words "Teleplay by Howard Prince" appeared, the Friendly Tavern filled with applause.

Meyer's wife looked at her husband, who was still eating. "Your brother, *Howard?*" she asked, with disbelief.

Meyer shrugged. "With writers, it takes awhile to find yourself."

Alfred waited until all the credits had been shown before switching off his set. It hurt him not to see his own name on the screen when the show was so good, but he was thankful that at least he was working.

He drained the glass of milk and stood up. It was time to go to work.

The telephone in the studio control room rang endlessly.

"Studio twelve," Florence kept saying happily. She was prepared for congratulations and she got them every time. "Yes, I thought so, too. It was terrific. . . . Thank you."

She hung up and swept back her long black hair. The show had been even better than she had expected; she wondered if Howard had liked it.

The telephone rang again.

"Studio twelve."

It was Tom Hampton. He asked to speak to the producer.

Florence held the receiver out to Sussman. "God," she whispered.

"Hello," Sussman said, self-importantly. "Why, thank you. Thank you very much." He grinned, in spite of himself. "Yes, I'll tell everyone. . . . Thank you."

He hung up. The telephone rang again but this time they ignored it.

"I think we've got a winner," Sussman said.

Six

The Oyster Bar at the Plaza Hotel was jammed. Howard and Florence sat at a table by the window, with a view of Fifty-ninth Street. Pretty girls in long dresses hurried along in the early spring sunshine. Long sleek cars moved effortlessly through traffic. The sky was blue, the air clear, the world beautiful.

Their lunch—oysters Rockefeller, fresh sole sautéed in butter, endive salad—all carefully ordered by Howard, was excellent. The bottle of Pouilly-Fuissé was nearly empty, and both of them felt the effects of the icy wine. They looked at each other, oblivious of the traffic and conversation around them, and of the headwaiter's desire to give their table to waiting customers.

"Did you always want to be a writer?" Florence asked. For the last half-hour she had been trying to draw Howard out, but with little success.

"Always," said Howard, as he poured out the last of the wine. The success of "Grand Central" had given

41

him confidence. His ten percent of the money had enabled him to pay off the rest of his debts. He felt free and strong, in his element, entertaining a beautiful, classy girl. It was what he had always dreamed about.

"How come you started so late?" Florence asked. She had never met anyone quite like Howard. He seemed so basic.

"You can't be a writer without having lived," he said.

"Well, there's also the life of the mind . . ."

"Life is experience," Howard went on. He had already practiced this answer. "I had to get that experience before I could write."

Florence swirled the wine about in her glass, and gazed down into it. "Did you get a lot of experience?"

She sounded almost sad.

"The usual—bummed around. Seaman, boxer . . ." Howard tried to think of another romantic profession. Neither cashier nor bookie fit his new image. "What you have to do to be a writer."

He tossed off his wine. Florence smiled at him, intrigued. His bravado was charming and, as far as she was concerned, unnecessary. His view of the profession was, she thought, childlike.

"You don't believe me," he said.

"Should I?"

She was smarter than he thought.

"Well," he said, "I bummed around, you can believe that. How about you?"

"Not a lot," she said dryly.

"I didn't mean it that way."

"It's a legitimate question," she said.

Other girls Howard knew were not so natural about sex. They might like it, but they never *talked* about it.

THE FRONT

"I mean," he said, retreating, "where are you from?"

"Connecticut." Florence sat up very straight. "Very proper family, very well-bred. The kind of family where the biggest sin was to be rude to the servants."

"In my family, the biggest sin was to buy retail."

Florence laughed, covering her mouth with her napkin.

"What's so funny?" he asked. He had been serious.

"You're so . . ." She paused, and said sweetly, "So unexpected."

Howard wanted to kiss her right there in the Oyster Bar. But he didn't have the nerve.

"I didn't expect you, either," he admitted.

After dropping Florence off at the studio, Howard rode the crowded subway back to Brooklyn. He was enchanted with her. Such a girl, from a well-to-do suburban family, would have been beyond the reach of a poor boy from DeKalb Avenue if it hadn't been for Alfred's script. Not only had Florence grown up buying retail, but she also had class and brains. If Howard hoped to make it with her, he would have to improve his role as a writer.

He left the subway and walked to Bert's secondhand bookstore, off Flatbush Avenue. He often went there, not to buy books, but to receive bets from Bert, the bearded owner and an old friend.

For the next half-hour, Howard and Bert walked up and down the dimly lit, musty-smelling aisles, looking for books. Howard didn't want to admit that he needed advice, so he asked for "bargains."

"How about Dickens?" Bert asked, blowing dust off a row of old volumes. "You need any Dickens?"

"I still got *David Copperfield* from high school. And *Tale of Two Cities.*"

Bert was incensed. "You were supposed to give them back when we graduated."

"So they're overdue." Howard always paid his debts. Some just took longer than others. "How about Russians? You got a secondhand *War and Peace?*"

Bert poked among the shelves. "I'm all out right now. You want a *Brothers Karamazov?*"

"Okay." Howard wondered if writers could be blacklisted for reading Russian authors.

"You ought to have some Mark Twain," Bert told him.

Howard snorted. "That's for kids."

"You call yourself a writer? Modern American writing started with *Huckleberry Finn,* dummy."

"It did?"

Howard wished he had paid more attention in English class.

"Hemingway said that," Bert explained. "How about Hemingway?" He checked out the stack of books that Howard held under one arm. "You're low on moderns —Faulkner, Sherwood Anderson . . ."

"Give me a Hemingway and two Faulkners."

Bert pulled the books down and Howard added them to his load. He began to edge toward the door.

"Remember, you got to pay for these, Howard. No credit."

But Howard was already headed for the street.

"Don't worry," he called.

He'd pay Bert just as soon as he borrowed more money from Meyer.

"How can you be broke?"

Meyer stood over his desk, in full view of his employees through the plate-glass window in his office wall. His face was bright pink, his hands shook, and he had trouble breathing. And all because Howard had made a simple request.

"How can you be broke?" Meyer repeated.

Howard shrugged. It was easy to be broke after eating lunch at the Oyster Bar.

"You just got a big paycheck. Don't tell me it wasn't a thousand, fifteen hundred . . ."

"I'm still an unknown," Howard said.

"What am I talking about?" Meyer was shouting. "Five thousand, probably. You're making as much as I am!"

"That's how much you know. There's agents, taxes." Howard shifted his load of secondhand books. "I got to buy books, paper . . ."

Meyer sat heavily in his plush swivel chair. "Money goes through you like Epsom salts. You're a sick individual."

"I'll pay you back," Howard promised. He needed money for new clothes, new furniture, a new apartment. Most of all, he needed money for Florence. "I just sold a new script."

The news made Meyer even angrier. "Don't play me for a sucker."

Meyer didn't know Howard only got ten percent of the money for a script. Howard couldn't tell him.

"I didn't make a business having the fur pulled over my eyes," Meyer said, unaware of his own pun.

Howard agreed.

"I'm nobody's fool."

"Of course not," said Howard.

"I'm glad you're finally realizing yourself, but not at my expense." Meyer shook his head. "A man earns, and still he borrows?"

Howard said nothing.

Meyer came around the desk and held the door

open. "First you pay back what you owe," he said.

That night, cashiering at the Friendly Tavern, Howard had an idea. He knew how he could get more money without having to borrow from anybody.

He left the tavern late and headed for the subway. He walked quickly, the collar of his windbreaker turned up, his hands thrust deep in his pockets. Few people were on the street, but Howard moved furtively; he didn't want to be recognized. He ducked into the arcade off Flatbush and descended the subway stairs two at a time.

Catching an uptown train, he hunched in a corner of the seat watching the stations fly past, dimly lit, almost deserted. At Sheridan Square, he bolted from the train and climbed the stairs to the bright lights and crowded pavements of Greenwich Village. Couples strolled in and out of the bars, trailed by the cool sounds of the new modern jazz. The faces were all unfamiliar here and Howard relaxed a little. But he didn't slow down.

He entered the apartment building on Macdougal Street, carefully read the names above the mailboxes, then pushed a pearly button. The buzzer sounded and Howard pushed open the door into the lobby.

The elevator took him to the fifth floor. He stepped quickly out into the narrow hallway and knocked on a lacquered black door. It opened immediately.

"Right on time," Alfred said. "I just finished."

Howard followed him into the study. It was cluttered with typewriter paper, used coffee cups, and cigarette butts. Crumpled paper spilled from the wastebasket onto the floor. More paper was stacked in the center of Alfred's desk.

"Want a drink?" Alfred asked.

"Okay." Howard could use some extra fortitude before he put forth his new idea.

Alfred went to the liquor cabinet. Dressed in pajamas and a wrinkled terry-cloth robe, his hair was uncombed and there were dark blotches beneath his eyes. The strain of long hours over the typewriter showed in the lines about his mouth.

"You look tired," Howard said.

"This was a hard one." Alfred handed him a glass of Scotch. "Shit, they're all hard. But it turned out good, I think."

"You really work hard, don't you?" Howard had never really thought about it. To him, writing was a kind of typing. "It's awful, that blacklist. You having to work like this."

Alfred laughed. "I always worked like this."

He took a bottle of Gelusil from the pocket of his robe, opened it, and turned the bottle up. The Gelusil coated his stomach, keeping the liquor he was about to drink from attacking his ulcer. Now Alfred held up his own glass of Scotch and offered a toast.

"To work," he said.

Howard wasn't sure he wanted to drink to work, but he turned up his glass anyway. It was time to bring up his new idea.

"There must be a lot of writers blacklisted by now," he said casually. "How do they get along?"

Alfred lowered his glass, suspicious. "Why?"

Howard shrugged. "It must be hard."

"It's hard," Alfred agreed.

Howard went to the desk and began to flip through the pages of the new script he was to deliver to Sussman. He pretended to read it.

"You know," Howard said suddenly, as if the idea

had just occurred to him, "I got them so snowed. . . . Two writers wouldn't be any harder than one."

Alfred was noncommittal. "You think not?"

"What do you have to know?" Howard asked, a little defensively. "It's a snap."

Alfred said dryly, "How about three?"

"Even three."

"At ten percent each." Alfred had gotten the point right off the bat.

"Well," Howard said, "maybe I could do three for twenty-five."

"I wouldn't want you to feel cheated." Alfred's sarcasm was cutting.

"Okay," Howard readily agreed. "Ten percent each."

Alfred shook his head.

"You don't think that's fair?"

"It's a bargain." Alfred took a deep drink of Scotch.

"I got the time; you know the writers who need help. I'm willing to help."

"Cut the crap, Howard."

"It means a lot of running around," Howard insisted. "You know, cabs, lunches. . . . I got to keep up appearances."

"You want the money."

"I'm offering a deal! What are you, romantic? That's the trouble with you leftos. . . ." Howard would just have to help Alfred help himself. "You got a thing about money. You want the deal or don't you want it?"

"I want it, but I know you."

Howard said philosophically, "Money is a tool. It's what you use it for."

"You're going to take off," Alfred warned, "and fly right up your own ass."

But Howard was elated. He took Alfred by the shoulders and gave him a friendly shake.

"Take advantage!" he said.

That was Howard's motto.

Seven

Howard met the new writers at Greenberg's Dairy Restaurant on Bleecker Street. Most of the customers were students from New York University who took little notice of the four men huddled together at a back table, two of them holding manila envelopes.

The two writers were Herb Delany, a lean, stoop-shouldered political activist with a brusque manner, and Bill Phelps, an easygoing, professorial type in horn-rimmed glasses. They were both eager to use Howard as a front.

"All I can say, Howard," Bill Phelps began after Alfred had made the introductions, "is thanks."

"It's no trouble," Howard said.

"I'm a Communist, Howard," Delany told him. "I want you to know that, right off the bat."

Alfred had already explained that Delany had been called before the House Committee on Un-American Activities and that he had refused to testify. Delany was known as a "Fifth-Amendment Commie."

"The Committee asked me," Delany went on, proud of what he had done. "I took the Fifth. None of their business. But I'm telling you."

"Listen, it's none of *my* business." In fact, Howard wasn't interested in Delany's politics.

"I just want you to know who you're fronting for."

"I don't have to know." Howard didn't *want* to know.

"What about taxes?" Phelps asked, changing the subject. "That's going to be a problem."

The waiter, arriving with their food, overheard Phelps's question.

"You need a deductible," the waiter advised, setting his tray on the table. "Take my advice—natural gas."

"I heard cattle," said Howard.

"Cattle is also good."

The three writers looked at one another. Howard, it seemed, had big plans for his ten percent.

"Fillet of sole," said the waiter, dealing out the plates. "Vegetable cutlet. Mushroom omelet. Protose steak. Eat in good health."

When he was gone, Alfred nodded toward Howard. "The network pays him," he said. "He pays us, less ten percent. We pay all the taxes we owe. No tricks, nothing illegal. Everyone declares exactly what he earns."

Delany saw a problem. "What's he paying us for? He's got to put something down."

"We're his collaborators."

Phelps shook his head. "Anyone reads his return, they connect him to us. Can't we protect him better?"

"The IRS won't care as long as the right tax is being paid."

"The FBI will," Phelps said. "And they've been looking at tax returns."

"For political reasons. Howard's not political."

That was an understatement. Howard had listened to the conversation with growing amazement.

"You guys kill me," he said finally. "They're kicking your brains in and you worry about taxes."

"We're worrying about you," Alfred said, annoyed. Phelps and Delany nodded.

"Just write the scripts," Howard told them. "I'll handle my end."

Francis X. Hennessy left the elevator and walked down the corridor toward the offices of the Freedom Information Service. Chin up, shoulders back, the latest volume of Committee testimony under one arm, he ignored the man who followed him, begging for attention. He was a middle-aged actor whose name had been added to the list of those suspected of being sympathetic to Communism.

Hennessy had never seen the actor before. He didn't like the man's theatrical good looks, or the dramatic quality of his voice, now choked with emotion. But his desperation excited Hennessy. He loved to see Commies crawl.

"But I'm Harry Stone, the *actor*," the man pleaded. "It's the other Harry Stone, the director—he's the one you want." He touched Hennessy's arm, imploring him to listen. "I'm blacklisted because you think I'm him."

Hennessy turned, his hand resting on the door handle. He didn't like to appear unreasonable.

"I understand," he said.

"I'm innocent," whispered the actor. "I never joined anything. A terrible mistake has been made."

"I sympathize."

The actor broke into an uncertain smile of gratitude. Hennessy knew that expression well.

"Unfortunately," Hennessy added, "I can only help people who are willing to make a clean breast of what they've done."

"But I haven't done anything!"

"That's why I can't help you."

Hennessy stepped into the office and shut the door in Harry Stone's face.

"Mr. Hampton called from the network," the receptionist said. "He wants you to call back as soon as you can."

"Get him."

Hennessy marched into his own office. Spread out on his desk was a freshly typed report of the investigation of the network's star writer. Hennessy wasn't pleased with the results of that investigation so far.

The telephone rang. It was Tom Hampton.

"Yes, Tom," Hennessy said. "I've got a report on Howard Prince."

Hampton asked if Howard was a member of the Communist party.

"No, no proof he's a member," Hennessy said reluctantly. "No proof that he isn't. I suggest we keep investigating."

Hampton wanted to know if that was necessary.

"No, I don't have to keep at it. I can send you a bill right now and forget it." Hennessy would never do that, but he knew how to handle these executives. "You're the one who has to answer to the American people."

Hampton immediately became defensive. If there was a chance that Howard Prince was a Communist, he said, then the investigation should continue.

"That's all I'm saying." Hennessy was pleased. "You can't be too careful these days."

Hampton asked if there was any objection to using Howard's scripts while the investigation was going on.

"No, I don't suppose anyone can object if you keep using him. Nothing to object to." Hennessy paused, and added, "So far."

Tom Hampton hung up, and gave a sigh of relief. He was a brittle man with a salt-and-pepper mustache and a strong instinct for survival. That instinct extended to his management of the network. Hampton had a responsibility to the shareholders; he had to make sure the network's reputation was not harmed and advertisers scared away. The Freedom Information Service and Francis X. Hennessy and his friends had the power to scare them away. Whether or not the actors and writers who were placed on the blacklist were actually guilty didn't concern Tom Hampton. They were replaceable. The network's profits were not.

"You can use him," he told Sussman, who sat anxiously on the other side of Hampton's desk.

"Thank God," Sussman said. "He's the best writer I've got. Hell, he's the *only* writer."

Neither Sussman nor Hampton wanted to lose Howard Prince. The ratings for "Grand Central" were skyrocketing, and Howard seemed to turn out scripts with the speed and efficiency of a machine.

"I don't know how he does it," added Sussman with admiration.

Hampton didn't care how he did it, just so long as he kept up the good work and kept off Hennessy's list.

"What about Hecky Brown?" asked Sussman.

Hampton shook his head. Hecky was definitely blacklisted.

"But he wrote the letter."

"Wasn't good enough," Hampton said.

Sussman was disappointed and a little disgusted.

"It's not my decision, Phil," Hampton added and made a vague reference to the board of directors. "They tell me, and I tell you."

"And what do I tell Hecky?"

"You decided he's not right for the part. You're changing the character." That was Sussman's problem. "You've fired actors before. Tell him what you told them."

"He'll know it's not true."

"Can he prove it?" Hampton asked.

After all, that was what really mattered.

Eight

Howard worked the lunch hour at the Friendly Tavern for the last time. When the rush was over, everyone gathered round to wish him luck. Margo handed him a notebook covered in pigskin with Howard's initials embossed in gold on the cover, a token of their affection.

"For your thoughts," Margo said, "when you want to write them down."

Howard was touched. He didn't know what to say, so he kissed Margo on the lips. Then he kissed her again.

"When you got a minute, Howard." Nat, the owner, drew him to one side. "I have an idea for a series. About a restaurant, you know? All you got to do is write it up. It's a natural!"

"Not easy getting a show on, Nat."

"With your name on it?" Nat winked. He knew

Howard could get anything on television if he wrote the script.

The bartender tapped Howard on the shoulder. "Can I get something down on the Boston–Yankees series?"

"Who do you want?"

"The Yankees."

"How much?" Howard asked. He would never be too successful to get a bet down.

"Fifty."

Howard opened his new notebook and listed the bet. He had already found a use for his present.

"You're down," he told the bartender.

April sunshine warmed the bleak, gray stones of the Cloisters, up in the Bronx. Howard and Florence sat close together on a bench, surrounded by trees with new leaves and emerging daffodils, with a view of the Palisades of New Jersey across the Hudson. A barge churned downriver, loaded with garbage, while the water reflected a clear blue sky. The sounds of traffic from the West Side Highway barely reached them.

He kissed her, long and passionately. Holding her close, he realized she was trembling.

"You need a fur coat?" Howard asked. He wanted to do something nice for Florence.

"No." She was surprised by the offer.

"I can get you a great buy."

"You don't need to get me things," she said, looking up at him.

"It's no trouble. My brother's a furrier."

Florence seemed puzzled so Howard kissed her again. They got along very well when they were kissing, but conversation was sometimes difficult.

"I should be getting back to the office," Florence said.

"What's the rush? You're having a script conference. That takes time."

"Then we should talk about the script."

"Later." Howard thought Florence was too idealistic. He tried to kiss her again, but she turned away. "What's the matter?" he asked.

"You're the only writer I know who never wants to talk about his work."

"I'm superstitious."

"No," she said, gently rebuking him, "you're not."

"Well, the way I look at it, you're a writer or you're a talker."

"You're genuinely modest." Florence thought she had discovered something about Howard at last, something definite. "I admire you for that."

"Listen," Howard said, changing the subject, "how do you feel about sports?"

"I'm embarrassing you."

"You like sports?" he persisted.

"I like swimming."

"Swimming's not a sport." He felt confident talking about sports. "Swimming is what you do so you shouldn't drown. A sport is what you do with a ball."

"I used to play basketball at school."

"You played basketball? Maybe we should play one-on-one sometime."

Florence didn't think the joke was very funny.

"No, listen," said Howard, "if you ever want to lay a bet . . ."

This time she laughed, in spite of herself.

"No," Howard said, flustered, "forget that. Listen . . ." He suddenly wanted to tell her the truth about himself. "I'm not just a writer. I don't want you to think . . ." He wasn't sure what he wanted her to think. What if she only liked him as a writer? "As a matter of fact . . ." He tried to get up the courage to say it. "I want you to know . . ."

"I know," Florence said.

Howard panicked. "You know?"

"How I feel about you."

"That's what you know?" he asked, relieved.

"I don't have to know anything more."

And Florence kissed him again.

Two FBI agents parked their unmarked Ford coupe on Christopher Street, with a clear view of the entrance to the brownstone apartment building. They tipped their hats low on their foreheads and settled back to wait. Both agents were well-dressed, and wore raincoats buttoned all the way up to their ties. They ignored the people who strolled past their car—the girls in long duffel coats left over from the winter, the bearded beatniks in dungarees. They kept their eyes glued for their quarry.

Herb Delany came out of the apartment building, carrying a manila envelope. He looked up and down the street, then started walking in the agents' direction. They quickly got out of the car and crossed the pavement.

Delany didn't see them until they were standing on either side of him.

"Mr. Delany?" said one.

Delany looked around. The other agent had flipped open his wallet.

"Federal Bureau of Investigation," he said. "We'd like to talk to you."

They were polite, but firm.

"I've got nothing to say," Delany said and kept walking.

The first agent blocked his way, casually, but effectively.

"We thought you might be ready to cooperate," he said.

Both agents smiled, as if they were as much victims as Delany was.

He pushed past them and walked on. There was a tightness in his throat and his mouth was dry.

Then Delany saw Howard. He was headed down from Seventh Avenue, toward the apartment building, to meet Delany. There was no time to warn him. Delany walked faster, hoping that Howard wouldn't see him. But Howard stopped in the middle of the sidewalk and smiled—a big, open sign of recognition.

Delany walked past him, without glancing to either side. "Keep walking," he said in a low, urgent voice.

Puzzled, Howard did as he was told. He didn't even notice the two men in raincoats and hats standing beside their Ford coupe.

But they noticed him.

Nine

Howard stepped out of the cab in front of the studio, carrying Bill Phelps's latest script under his arm. He tipped the driver a dollar and pushed through the revolving door. The elevator operator in his crisp blue uniform nodded deferentially. Secretaries showed him big, toothy smiles. Howard was a star.

He stepped off the elevator on the sixth floor and walked jauntily into Sussman's office.

Sussman's secretary shouted, "You're here!"

Howard bowed. That was the kind of reception he liked.

"He's here," the secretary repeated into the intercom. Then she told Howard, "We've been trying all over."

Sussman came charging out of his office. "Thank God," he said, grabbing Howard's arm.

"I said I'd bring it in today." Howard held out the manila envelope.

"Forget that one," said Sussman, taking the envelope and tossing it onto the secretary's desk.

"Forget it?"

Sussman pushed him toward the door. "You've got to rewrite the old one."

"What old one?" There were so many.

"The one with the flashbacks to the concentration camp."

Howard hadn't read that one either. "You said it was great."

"It's beautiful."

Sussman led him hurriedly down the corridor.

"Florence said she cried," Howard added.

"An award-winning show. Those scenes in the gas chamber . . ." Sussman thumped his chest. "*I* cried!"

"Then what . . ."

"The sponsor won't approve it."

Sussman led the way into the rehearsal studio. The sets for the show were all arranged, the actors sitting on folding chairs, in costume, waiting for the rehearsal to get under way. Everyone looked expectantly at Howard.

Florence ran up, all smiles, clutching the shooting script. "You found him," she said happily.

Howard didn't share her elation. He knew trouble when he saw it.

Sussman explained about the sponsor. "First they said yes, now they say no. Right when we're ready for dress rehearsal. You want to know why? You won't believe it."

"They're a gas company," Florence said. "They decided that the show makes gas look bad."

Florence and Sussman began to laugh, but Howard didn't think it was so funny.

"I still think we can make it a firing squad," Sussman suggested. "After all, they killed Jews that way, too."

Florence watched Howard's face grow dark. She figured he was angry because the sponsor was interfering with his creative work.

"Phil," she said softly, "will you leave it to Howard? He's the writer."

But Howard was grateful for Sussman's suggestion. "So they want changes. What's the excitement? Make it a firing squad. Good idea."

The problem was solved as far as Howard was concerned.

"You'll have to write new scenes," Florence said.

He took the shooting script from her. "I'll go home and write them."

"You don't have time to go home."

"I'll take a cab."

Sussman took Howard's arm. "You don't realize. Time is of the essence. They're waiting upstairs for the rewrite. The sponsor has to approve."

Howard edged toward the door, but Sussman held onto his arm. He smiled imploringly. "For the network. They don't approve, there's no show."

"Can't they wait till tonight?" Howard asked.

"They want it now. I'm supposed to keep you here till it's done."

Howard was desperate. "I can't work any place but home."

"We fixed you up an office. I guarantee you won't be disturbed."

"I don't get inspired!"

"It doesn't have to be inspired," Sussman said, "only changed."

Florence tried to be reassuring. "There really isn't

that much writing. We just have to be careful not to lose the emotion."

"Don't bother him with details. He has work to do."

With Sussman on one side and Florence on the other, Howard walked back down the corridor. Sussman pushed open the door of an unoccupied office. A new typewriter sat on the desk, with paper and pencils neatly arranged next to it, a sight that made Howard sick to his stomach.

Sussman and Florence waited for him to sit down at the desk and confront the tools of his trade.

"Just clear your mind," Sussman instructed, "and write."

Florence smiled encouragement. Then the two of them went out and closed the door, leaving Howard alone with his talent.

Howard rushed to the window to see if he could escape that way. But six floors was a long jump, even for someone in his predicament. There was no telephone and no way out except through the door. It seemed hopeless.

He opened the door and peered out into the corridor. Sussman and Florence stood talking next to the water cooler. They looked up expectantly.

"I have to go to the bathroom," Howard said.

Sussman pointed toward the end of the corridor. Howard walked past them, smiling, and into the men's room. He would wait there, to see if the two of them returned to the rehearsal studio.

An associate producer came out of one of the stalls. He nodded to Howard and Howard nodded back. When the man left, Howard leaned against the door, even more worried. What if Sussman needed to go to the bathroom?

He cracked open the door. Sussman and Florence

were gone. In an instant, he was out in the corridor, racing toward the fire exit. He had a chance, if he could only get to the stairs. There was a telephone in a corner of the downstairs lobby.

He rushed down the six flights and out into the lobby. The telephone booth was empty. He stepped quickly inside, turned his back to the bank of elevators, and began to search his pockets for change. What if he didn't have a nickel?

He found a coin, deposited it, and dialed Alfred's number. Then he closed his eyes and waited for the telephone to ring. It rang—and rang and rang. Why wasn't Alfred home, writing, like he was supposed to be?

Just as Howard was about to hang up, Alfred answered, sounding as if he'd come out of a sound sleep. Howard didn't bother with the amenities. He told Alfred what he had to do and hung up.

He took the steps back up to the sixth floor two at a time. The corridor was still empty. He raced along it and back into his office, where he slumped into his chair. He could barely catch his breath. His lungs hurt. Suddenly, he became aware of someone stopping on the other side of the door, listening. Howard grabbed a piece of paper and a pencil, furrowing his brow as if deep in thought.

Sussman looked in. "How's it coming?"

"Great," panted Howard.

"I didn't hear the typewriter."

"I start longhand."

Sussman withdrew. Howard got up and ran to the window. Forty-second Street was packed with traffic. Most of the cars were Yellow cabs, and Howard waited anxiously for one of them to deliver his savior.

An hour later Florence left the rehearsal studio to check on Howard's progress. She paused outside the door of his office, listening for the staccato voice of the typewriter. Florence equated that sound with genius and she wondered why she didn't hear it now. Howard must be deep in thought, struggling to create new scenes to satisfy a stupid, arbitrary sponsor. She wanted to offer him comfort, but her professionalism prevented her from interrupting him.

Poor, brilliant Howard, she thought, as she returned to the studio.

Howard, however, was not struggling to create anything. He was still struggling to spot Alfred in the street below. His face pressed to the window, he watched Yellow cab after Yellow cab pull up in front of the network building, until at last a tall, sandy-haired figure stepped out onto the pavement. Alfred!

Howard was out in the corridor again, running for the fire exit. In less than two minutes, he had reached the lobby. Alfred stood uncertainly on the pavement outside, some loose sheets of typewriter paper in one hand, staring up at the building. Howard ran through the revolving door and snatched the papers from him. Neither of them spoke. Alfred hurried back to the waiting cab; Howard ran inside the building.

This time he climbed the stairs one at a time, pausing on each landing to catch his breath.

Opening the fire door, he saw Sussman coming down the corridor. The producer paused outside the office where Howard was supposed to be working, and Howard knew it was all over now. Sussman would discover that he was not in the office. His career was finished, and so was his relationship with Florence. In a matter of minutes, she would know he was a phony.

But Sussman didn't go in. He continued on down the corridor, entering his own office.

Howard took several deep breaths, then followed him.

Sussman and Florence sat on either side of the big, mahogany desk. They broke into smiles at the sight of Howard. Florence got up, took the typewritten pages, and placed them in front of the producer. She and Sussman read the new scenes eagerly while Howard collapsed in a chair.

"That's how we treat talent," Sussman said, when he had finished reading. "Sometimes I'm ashamed."

Florence looked at Howard with loving admiration.

They left the studio together. Florence took Howard to her apartment on the Upper East Side, a spacious one-room efficiency filled with exotic plants and shelves of books from floor to ceiling. Her windows overlooked Central Park. They had a drink together, although it was still early afternoon, looking down at mothers pushing baby carriages around the pond and bicyclists crossing Sheep Meadow.

Howard was still unsettled by his narrow escape. He was unusually silent, hardly spoke even when he found himself on the couch with Florence.

Tenderly, they undressed each other.

Ten

Public School 161 had not changed much in fifteen years. The auditorium walls were still painted a sickly green and the windows apparently hadn't been washed since the night Howard was awarded his high-school diploma. Not that Howard minded, sitting on the stage above a sea of young, smiling faces. He was enjoying seeing the school as it had been. He had never dreamed, when he attended, that he would one day be returning as the pride of P.S. 161.

The principal stood at the corner of the stage, shouting orders, while teachers roamed the aisles, trying to quiet the students. The principal wore the same gray serge suit Howard remembered from his many encounters with him, and the same grimace. He still made Howard nervous.

"Quiet, children," the principal shouted. "Quiet!" He pointed to a rowdy kid in a leather jacket. "Send that boy to detention."

It sounded so familiar. Howard looked at the

teachers seated next to him on the stage. He knew most of them, including the one in the long flower-print dress who smiled at him. She had tried to teach Howard grammar, once hitting him with a ruler when the effort proved too much for body and mind.

"Quiet now! Everybody back in their seats!"

The assembly settled down and the principal began to speak in the voice he reserved for great occasions.

"Boys and girls, we have a very special visitor today. Not so long ago, he sat in the same seats you're sitting in now. But, because he worked hard and studied hard, he is now a famous television writer."

All eyes were on Howard Prince.

"Howard," the principal went on, holding up a certificate bearing a gold seal, "I know this prize we give you is a small thing compared to the greater prizes you have won in your chosen field. But it is an honor and a privilege as your former principal to present you with our highest award—Outstanding Graduate of P.S. 161!"

The auditorium filled with applause. The teachers on the stage stood and joined in, all of them beaming at Howard as he stepped forward to receive his prize.

Hecky Brown confronted himself in the dressing-room mirror. Rehearsal for the latest production in the "Grand Central" series was minutes away, yet the producer and the assistant producer were both here talking to Hecky. Sussman sat on one side of him, Florence on the other. Sussman made vague complaints about "Grand Central" while Florence maintained a disapproving silence.

Hecky felt uneasy. He carefully applied his makeup, grateful for the distraction. He wondered what the two of them were up to.

"What can I say?" Sussman finally asked, throwing up his hands. "I'm worried. And I'm not the only one. Upstairs . . ."

"From what?" Hecky said. "The show's a hit."

"So far."

"So far, so good."

"I have to look ahead. Your quality, I don't know what, the character . . ." Sussman floundered, searching for the right words. He didn't like having to lie and he didn't like having to do it in front of Florence. "It's not working."

Hecky dropped his eyebrow pencil. "You hired me for this character."

"The first impression . . ." Sussman countered. "Tremendous! Don't get me wrong."

Hecky turned to Florence. "You think, too?"

"I think you're great, Hecky." She seemed angry. "So does everyone else."

"It's not her decision," Sussman said quickly.

"What decision?"

Sussman ignored the question. "No one denies your talent. But you're a dominant personality. You belong out front . . . in a dramatic series. You're throwing the whole show off-balance."

"Who says?" Hecky suddenly had butterflies in his stomach.

Sussman just wanted it to be over.

"A talent like yours . . . it needs room. You need a show of your own, where you can dominate. As a matter of fact, I've got a few ideas." Sussman stood up, anxious to go. "We'll make some time, kick them around."

Hecky asked, "Is it the letter?"

"Absolutely not," said Sussman, too quickly.

Hecky knew it was the letter. "I wrote what he asked."

"Wouldn't I tell you? The problem is artistic."

Florence couldn't stand the hypocrisy any longer. Why couldn't Sussman tell Hecky the truth, that he had been blacklisted? It was so much better than lying. These obvious lies made her feel like part of the conspiracy.

She walked out of the dressing room, slamming the door behind her.

"The female of the species," Sussman joked.

But Hecky just stared at him in the mirror.

Florence returned to her office just long enough to get her coat. She was angry and confused, and she couldn't stand to remain in the studio or anywhere inside the network building.

She rode the elevator down without speaking to anyone, crossing Forty-second Street to the Nedicks on the corner. The man at the counter gave her change and she went to the telephone to call Howard. She had to tell someone about what they were doing to Hecky.

They met in Central Park, next to the pond. Howard knew something was wrong as soon as he saw Florence. Her lovely mouth was twisted and there were angry tears in her eyes. He listened quietly while she told him about the scene in the dressing room.

"I should have stayed, Howard," she concluded. "I was a coward, running out like that."

"You did what you could." Howard didn't like to dwell on misfortune. Hecky was just unlucky.

"Then I should quit." Florence sounded like she meant it. "I shouldn't stay there and be a good German."

"If you quit, you'll be out of work."

"I've been out of work before." She was determined. "I'll get along."

Howard felt protective. He put his arms around her. "You have to be practical."

"Practical is wrong! Practical is what people hide behind."

He was no match for her idealism.

"Florence, let's go home."

"You just want to screw." She pushed him away. "That's all you care about—writing and screwing."

It didn't seem like such a bad routine to Howard.

"And I can't write," she said, suddenly appealing for help. "I'm artistic without being talented. But you're both, Howard. You're an artist."

"What's that got to do with it?" he asked, warily.

"People will listen to you."

"Forget about me." Howard couldn't help Hecky even if he wanted to. He had a responsibility to Alfred and to the other writers he was supporting. "They'll listen to you, too. But not if you quit."

He didn't want her to ruin her career. There was nothing worse than being on the outside. Howard knew because he had been on the outside all of his life, until he became Howard Prince, the writer.

"Take my word for it," he said, "you can do more on the inside."

"Like I could do for Hecky?"

"Stop blaming yourself. I admit it's terrible, but . . ." He didn't know what to say.

"But what? Why is there always a but? If it's terrible, why can't we do something?"

"You want to do something, you got to be where it counts." Howard gently raised her chin. "On the inside."

"I don't know if I can take it, Howard."

"Sure you can." He kissed her. "You got an influence on Sussman; he listens to you. If you quit, who'd pay attention?"

Florence didn't answer. She rested her head against his shoulder, knowing that she would have to make her own decision.

"You're out," Howard added, almost to himself, "and you're a nobody."

Florence snuggled closer. "That feels good," she whispered, "you holding me."

Cold gray clouds had moved across the sun, like curdled milk. The wind came up like a bad omen, pushing the tiny sailboats too fast over the dark surface of the pond.

Eleven

Hecky sat in the inner office of the Freedom Information Service. He was pale and haggard, his round clown's face drawn into a tragic mask. He clasped his hands in his lap to keep them from trembling. Being fired by the network had sapped some of his confidence; but when he discovered no one else would hire him, he folded, shrunk, became terrified. The famous Hecky Brown was suddenly a nobody. The speed of the blacklisting process frightened him almost as much as its effectiveness.

Francis X. Hennessy sat across the desk from Hecky, reading the letter that Hecky had sent him. Hennessy's crew cut looked like a stiff brush.

"I wrote I was sorry," Hecky said, "that I was duped. I didn't know what I was doing. I'll never do it again."

But Hennessy didn't look up.

"What more can I say?"

Hennessy said offhandedly, "That's up to you."

"I have to work!" Hecky's voice broke.

This time Hennessy looked up. His deep blue, emotionless eyes fixed on Hecky's but he didn't speak.

"I can't work, Mr. Hennessy," Hecky pleaded. "The doors are closed in my face. My own agent won't answer the phone."

He pulled out a handkerchief and mopped his face. He felt nauseous.

"I appreciate your situation," Hennessy said. He sat back and pressed his fingertips together. "I do, Mr. Brown. I've helped people in your situation."

"Then help me, please. Tell me. I'll turn myself inside out; I'll do anything."

"You make that difficult to believe."

"What else can I do?" Hecky was desperate. "I'll do it, believe me. You don't know what I'm going through."

"I'd like to believe you." Hennessy never seemed to blink. "But I have the feeling you're not being entirely frank."

"Give me a for instance, that's all," Hecky said, anxious to prove himself. "You'll see, I promise."

Hennessy had Hecky Brown exactly where he wanted him. "You marched in the May Day Parade," he prompted.

"Only because of that girl."

"Whose name you can't remember."

"Tessie, Bessie . . ." Hecky really couldn't recall what she was called. "I was interested in her body, not her name."

"Other people marched in that parade," Hennessy said. "Actors, directors. You don't remember their names, either?"

"I'm terrible with names."

Hennessy decided to switch tactics.

"They remember you," he said.

"I'm a well-known personality." Hecky thought a moment, then asked, "You talked with these people?"

"Some of them. Some were kind enough to write letters." Hennessy made it sound like a charitable act.

"Then you know who they are. So it's not so important I remember. You know already."

He thought he saw a trace of annoyance in Hennessy's stonelike expression. What did the man want?

"Your sincerity is important," Hennessy said, soothingly. "Your desire to cooperate fully."

"I told you what I did. I apologized. I come on my hands and knees, Mr. Hennessy. Please, all I want to do is work. I don't want to know from anything else."

But apologies weren't enough. Hennessy knew that Hecky didn't really repent. True repenters complimented Hennessy and the work of the Freedom Information Service. They offered to help in the struggle.

"I've got a wife and two growing children," Hecky said. "Fine boys. Here, look . . ." He flipped through his wallet to color snapshots taken the summer before at Jones Beach. The sight of those pictures made Hecky want to cry, but Hennessy looked at the snapshots without a change of expression.

Hecky replaced his wallet. "Plus a wife from before," he went on, "who, if the first of the month the alimony doesn't come. . . . Last week I sold my car for peanuts —a brand-new model. . . . All the money I made, I ask myself, where did it go? So fast? I owe taxes you wouldn't believe. I can't pay the rent, Mr. Hennessy. Nothing can go out if it isn't coming in!"

Hennessy listened patiently to Hecky's list of woes. Then, out of the blue, he asked, "Do you know Howard Prince?"

Hecky was caught off guard. "I was on his show. A big talent . . . big."

Hennessy knew all about Howard Prince being a big talent—too big.

"Do you know him personally?"

"Only from the show," Hecky said, carefully weighing his words. "Once in a while, a bite to eat afterward."

"Do you think you could get to know him better?"

Hecky had been afraid of this. He couldn't bring himself to betray a friend.

"I'm not too good at that sort of thing, honest. Actors aside, you'd be surprised. They're really very shy."

"He knows you already," Hennessy persisted, leaning across the desk. "You're very likable. And I'm sure he feels sympathy for you."

So Howard Prince was also suspect. Hecky suddenly realized no one was safe.

"What could I find out?" Hecky asked.

"Who his friends are. What he does in his spare time. Where he stands on the issues of the day."

"Can't you ask him that yourself?"

Hennessy allowed himself a thin smile. These people were such fools.

"If he were part of the Communist conspiracy," he said, "could we believe what he said?"

"But if he isn't?"

"We'd like you to help us find out."

Hecky said reluctantly, "You want me to spy on Howard Prince." No one seemed less like a Communist.

Hennessy swept Hecky's letter to one side. "We're in a war, Mr. Brown," he said with sudden forcefulness, his blue eyes flashing, "against a tricky and ruthless enemy who will stop at nothing to destroy our way of life. To be a spy on the side of freedom is an honor."

Hecky knew Howard didn't want to destroy the American way of life. He was too busy enjoying it.

"And I do that," he said, making sure. "I can work?"

"I don't do the hiring, Mr. Brown. I only advise about Americanism."

Hennessy sat back in his chair and pressed his finger-tips together again. His face was flushed, his expression triumphant. He studied Hecky for a moment, like a general evaluating his field position.

"But in my opinion," Hennessy said, "as the sign of a true patriot, it would certainly help."

Hecky's mission was clear.

Twelve

Howard sat beneath hot studio lights on the set of a television talk show called "Manhattan." The interviewer—a drama critic wearing a narrow bow tie—talked eagerly about Howard's scripts as Howard turned his chair from side to side, watching himself on the monitor. This was his first television appearance and he was totally relaxed. Why shouldn't a television writer feel at home on television? He admired his new, tailor-made jacket and his hair that was recently cut by a "stylist" rather than a barber. Howard decided that he looked as successful as he felt.

The interviewer smiled. "Well, I would think one of the factors that has made your show so successful . . ."

But Howard raised his hand in protest. "Don't call it my show. I'm just a cog in the wheel."

"The most important cog, in my opinion."

Howard grinned. He couldn't argue with a drama critic.

"I think one can safely say," the interviewer continued, "that 'Grand Central' is one of the few television shows where the writer is really the star."

"Well, there's a lot of wonderful people who work on that show." Howard wanted to be fair.

"Of course. I understand the importance of actors and directors . . ."

"And the producer," Howard added. "Without Phil Sussman . . ."

"Still, wouldn't you say it all rests on the writer? Ultimately?"

"Well, naturally, the script comes first," Howard admitted. "You can't have a show without a script."

"So, to come back to what I started to say . . ."

"Please," Howard said. He didn't want any credit not due him, no matter how great his talent.

"The wide range of styles in 'Grand Central,' comedy one week, tragedy the next . . ."

"We try to mix it up."

"Don't you find that difficult, switching from one style to another?"

"Not at all," said Howard. Nothing could have been easier.

"Most writers are known as comedy writers or dramatic writers. You seem at home in almost any style you try."

"I just write, that's all." Howard shrugged. "What comes out, comes out."

The interviewer nodded sagely, as if Howard had said something of great significance.

Hecky watched the interview from the bar in Toots Shor's restaurant. He sat alone, nursing a Scotch and soda, listening to Howard with combined envy and despair. He thought he would feel comfortable at Toots's. He had spent a lot of money there over the years and the bartender was still a friend. But Hecky detected a coolness on the part of the other actors and show-business people who moved gaily between the bar and the restaurant.

The "Manhattan" show concluded with a flattering head shot of Howard smiling into the camera. The bartender switched off the television set and Hecky looked up to see Tom Hampton and his wife coming through the door. Hecky considered them to be friends of his. Hampton had once been very eager for Hecky to sign a contract with the network. Hecky had enlivened several Hampton dinner parties.

Hampton's wife saw him and smiled. She started toward him, and Hecky climbed off the stool to greet her.

He never got the chance. Hampton had seen him first, and skillfully guided his wife away, toward a waiting maître d'.

Howard loved his new apartment. Located on East Thirty-ninth Street, it enjoyed a panoramic view of the East River and the Fifty-ninth Street Bridge linking Manhattan to Queens. At night, the lights covering the bridge seemed to glow for his own private enjoyment.

He had furnished the apartment himself, picking the latest styles—a low couch the size of a bed, deep, sumptuous chairs, and patterned shag rugs an inch thick. The books from Bert's shop were neatly arranged in shelves on either side of the fireplace.

Howard was ready for Florence's first visit. The table was set for two, the champagne bottle nestled in a silver bucket of ice, wrapped in fresh linen. The smell of *coq au vin* drifted in from the kitchen. The cool, lazy chords of Dave Brubeck's piano issued from Howard's hi-fidelity set, the latest thing in sound. Indirect lighting—there were no more lampshades lined with tinfoil—suffused the whole apartment in a soft, intimate glow.

Howard wore his new cashmere V-neck sweater and white bucks. He was standing at the table, applying a match to the tall, elegant candles set in crystal sconces when the doorbell rang.

He crossed the living room and opened the door with a grand, sweeping gesture. Florence was about to see how the real Howard Prince lived.

She stood awkwardly on the threshold, holding a battered notebook. Her coat was undone, her hair wild. Howard looked at her and stopped smiling.

"I quit!" she said excitedly before he could speak. "Quit, quit, finished, resigned. Quit!"

She swept past him into the apartment, dumping her notebook and coat on the couch. She didn't even look around.

"Let Sussman do his own dirty work," she said. "I won't be a part of it. No more, not any more. Finished! Watching those people destroyed, crucified like Hecky." She flopped down in one of the chairs, without being asked. "I'm going to fight it!"

Howard said, "Hi, Florence."

"I'm so relieved. You have no idea. I've felt like such a hypocrite—taking their money, keeping my mouth shut . . ."

"This is my new apartment." Howard gestured feebly.

But Florence didn't hear him. "They count on your silence, you know. People keeping quiet, afraid to speak up. But you know what I'm going to do?"

Howard shoved his hands into his pockets and

looked at the floor. There was nothing to do but wait until she had finished.

"I'm going to publish a newspaper—well, anyway, a pamphlet. 'Facts About Blacklist.' Do you like the title?" She didn't wait for him to answer. "I've been on the phone all day. People are dying to talk . . . as long as I don't use their names."

Florence was triumphant.

"Would you like some champagne?" Howard asked.

"We have to break the conspiracy of silence. People don't know what's going on. They don't have the facts. I've gotten pledges already for the printing costs—and volunteers to collect information. People will act if only they have the facts!"

"Let's not get hysterical."

"Oh, we'll shake them up, Howard." Her smile was radiant. "I'll do the leg work and you'll do the writing . . ."

"Not so fast," he said. She scared him with that kind of talk. "Florence, I think you're making a big mistake."

Florence had expected to be congratulated, not criticized.

"I believe in personal responsibility, Howard. If you believe, act!"

"You're throwing away a whole career."

"Thought without action," she said condescendingly, "is the disease of the liberal."

"You're the best story editor in the business. You could be a producer. . . ." He tried to think of something that would appeal to her idealism. "The first woman producer of a half-hour dramatic series in prime time."

"If I keep my mouth shut."

He said reasonably, "That is not such a terrible idea sometimes."

"That's what they're counting on!"

"Florence, listen to me. You are going off the deep end."

Florence was insulted and hurt. If she couldn't count on Howard, who could she count on? She turned her face away and bit her lip.

Howard went to the champagne cooler. He took the Dom Perignon '47 by the neck, wiped off the bottle with the napkin, and filled two glasses. The wine was full of bubbles, but somehow the fun had gone out of it. Depressed, he carried the glasses into the living room.

"Have some champagne," he said.

Florence took a glass, and downed half of it. He might as well have offered her Coca-Cola.

"I warned you," she said, "I'm a serious person."

"You're crazy." Howard was getting angry. "You quit your job; you're ready to start a revolution. What are you trying to do?"

"I want us to fight them, not get bought off."

"I'm not mad at anyone!" he shouted.

"We live in the world, Howard."

"You live in the world; I live right here." Howard had seen enough of the real world. "What are you trying to do to me? You know how long it took me to get here? I like it here! I like what I'm doing!"

"You're getting shrill," Florence said disapprovingly.

"I've got what I want." Why couldn't she accept that? "For the first time in my life . . ."

"I'm not trying to take it away from you."

"But that's what's gonna happen!"

Florence was hurt. Howard made it sound like she was interested in using *him,* not his talent.

She set her glass on the coffee table. "I'm only talking about a simple commitment, Howard. I didn't ask you to marry me."

The word "marry" surprised them both. It had never come up before.

Howard sat down beside her. "We got a good relationship going," he said. "Why do you want to spoil it?"

"A relationship isn't only sex, you know. There are more important aspects."

"I know there are." But Howard couldn't think of any.

"Like what?" he asked.

"Human rights."

"How about my rights?" he demanded. "I'm human. What happened to my rights all of a sudden?"

Florence couldn't understand how Howard could be so selfish. Writers were supposed to take chances.

"I live here," Howard said, indicating his new furniture, the apartment itself, and the view. "It's clean. What are you putting me on the spot for?"

"You really want success, don't you?"

Howard sighed. He looked out the window, toward the bread factory across the river in Queens. He had come a long way, and he wasn't going to let anything change that.

"I don't want to make waves," he admitted.

Florence stood and slipped into her coat.

"I'm a writer," Howard added, hoping that would make some difference.

Florence nodded. "I've made that mistake before, confusing the artist with the man. I just want you to know that I still admire the artist."

"You going?" Howard couldn't believe it. No ideal was that important.

"Yes."

He followed her to the door. Afraid she'd start crying, Florence rushed out without saying good-bye.

"Well then, go!" he shouted.

And he slammed the door so hard that his new bullfight poster swung crooked on the wall.

He dined alone on *coq au vin* in his new apartment. At first he felt deserted, self-righteous. Then he felt like a heel. Finally, he was just plain lonely.

He welcomed the ringing of the telephone. He answered it and a familiar voice said, "Howard? This is Hecky . . . Hecky Brown. Am I bothering you?"

"Of course not." Howard had always liked Hecky. He didn't want the man to feel rejected now that he was blacklisted. "I'm sorry about the show, Hecky. Everybody misses you."

Hecky thanked him. His voice was thick, as if he had been drinking too much.

"Howard," he said, "I'm calling for a favor. But I'll understand if you don't want to do it."

This was Howard's chance to prove his worth.

"Why shouldn't I do it?" he asked, knowing he should avoid anyone who was blacklisted.

"Well, you know how it is. You don't take anything for granted these days." Hecky didn't have to explain. "I've got this club date tomorrow in the mountains. I thought maybe you could drive me up."

Howard welcomed the diversion. "You couldn't have called at a better time," he said, thinking of Florence.

Thirteen

The trip to the Catskills was nothing new for Hecky—in the days before television, he had often played the nightclubs and mountain resorts. But there was no nostalgia attached to his return. Nowadays he had to take any job he could get, no matter how little it paid.

Howard drove since Hecky had a hangover and was on edge generally. The role of spy didn't agree with him.

Howard didn't seem to notice Hecky's nervousness. For him, the trip was an escape, an adventure. He'd never been north of Poughkeepsie and he imagined the mountains were full of girls, all waiting for him. But in spite of these happy fantasies, there was fakery to Howard's joviality. He couldn't stop thinking about Florence.

"When you work like I do," Howard boasted, while wheeling Hecky's secondhand Studebaker around the curves, "you got to make time to relax. You know, all work, and no play . . ."

"I guess you've got a lot of friends," Hecky said. That was one of the things Hennessy wanted to know.

"The usual." Howard tried to give the impression that he knew all the celebrities. "But you've got to hang loose—be able to pick up the phone, have a little fun, then get right back to basics."

Hecky grunted. He decided to plunge. "What do you like to do in your spare time?"

Howard smiled and raised his eyebrows.

"The usual," he said after a thoughtful pause. He meant sex.

Hecky settled back in the seat and closed his eyes. Spying on Howard was not going to be easy.

The hotel loomed ahead of them—a garish, prefabricated concrete structure sprawling at the highway's edge. Plaster statues of Greek deities lined the walkway from the parking lot to the main building. A pink awning over the door was painted with black, Gothic letters that proclaimed CATSKILL MANOR. The marquee advertised The Star-Lighters, not Hecky Brown.

"Watch your step around this place," Hecky warned. "The broads up here, you look at them and you think, where has this been? They're coming at you from all directions—like shooting fish in a barrel. Then you find out you're the fish."

It sounded just fine to Howard. "Don't worry about me."

"Just don't make any promises," Hecky said. "They come up here with lawyers."

Howard turned into the drive, pulling up beneath the awning. A long black limousine sat in front of them and Howard could see two girls with elaborate hairdos in the back seat.

"You play these places much?" Howard asked. The Catskill Manor didn't look good enough for the famous Hecky Brown.

Hecky said sadly, "Till I got into television." He didn't like remembering. "You know what I used to get for one night?"

Howard shook his head.

"Three grand."

"That ought to come in handy now."

"You know what I'm getting tonight?"

Howard thought he must be getting more.

"Five hundred," said Hecky, and he couldn't keep the bitterness out of his voice.

"That's not fair!" Howard hadn't realized the blacklist could reach so far.

"Where is it written it should be fair?"

Without waiting for an answer, Hecky climbed out of the car. A bellboy in a pink tunic approached, looking skeptically at the dilapidated Studebaker. Hecky opened the trunk for the boy to unload the two bags.

His arms out, a big smile on his face, a heavy-set man wearing sunglasses came out of the hotel. "Hecky," he called, waving, "it's a pleasure."

He hurried forward, expansive, and overly friendly. It was Sam, the owner.

"How long? A year? Two years?" He draped an arm around Hecky's shoulders, his suntan looking like it had been applied with a cotton swab. "It's a pleasure having you back."

"Likewise," said Hecky without enthusiasm. "Sam, this is Howard Prince, the great and famous writer."

"It's a pleasure, Howard." Sam pumped his hand. "Any friend of Hecky's."

But Howard was distracted by the girls in the limousine. One bellhop had unloaded several leather bags from the big car's trunk, while another pushed a dress rack forward and began to hang up dresses, pantsuits, robes, fur coats, and stoles. As Howard watched, the girls stepped out, and headed for the hotel. They both wore tight slacks and sunglasses, and seemed very available. The redhead smiled at him as she sauntered past.

"Come on," Sam said, "let's go inside and have a little drink."

"You know I don't drink before a show," Hecky reminded him.

"We'll have a little talk then."

Sam led them into the lobby, crowded with guests in loud but expensive clothes and heavy jewelry, all of them anxious for the evening to begin. They recognized Hecky instantly and a platinum blonde trailed him all the way to the front desk, asking for an autograph. Hecky joked, waved, and made his famous clownlike faces as he passed among his admirers. For the moment he seemed like his old, successful self— Hecky Brown, master comic. None of the guests realized what had happened to him.

While Hecky signed autographs, Howard looked over the prospects. He knew he was going to like the hotel, judging from the number of unattached women in view. He estimated the ratio of women to men at ten to one—the best odds he had ever enjoyed.

The redhead and her friend stood waiting by the elevators. The former had removed her sunglasses, revealing heavily made-up lashes and willing eyes. She smiled at Howard again, and he returned it in full.

"Staying long?" he asked.

"Just the weekend." She had a high-pitched, little-girl's voice that did not match her body. "You, too?"

Howard nodded and moved closer. This chick was a piece of cake.

"What do you do?" she asked.

"I'm a writer," he said proudly.

"A *writer?*"

Her smile turned into a grimace. She left him abruptly, stepping inside the elevator with her friend. They were giggling when the doors closed.

Howard saw that he had the wrong approach. These girls weren't interested in writers, only in men with steady, lucrative jobs. He would temporarily have to adopt a more conventional profession if he hoped to make out here.

Sam led Hecky and Howard into his office. It was lavishly furnished, though without taste, with wall-to-wall carpeting and a sofa covered in imitation fur. Photographs of Sam shaking hands with various entertainers covered the walls. Hecky's photograph was not among them.

Sam offered them chairs and stepped to the liquor cabinet. He poured Scotch from a decanter into two stemmed glasses and added ice cubes with silver tongs.

"You'll have a drink, Howard?"

"Sure."

Howard sipped some very good Scotch, enjoying his role as an insider.

Sam held up his own glass and toasted Hecky, "To a giant of the entertainment world."

Hecky knew Sam was trying to make up for paying him only five hundred dollars. He tried to return the gesture of courtesy.

"Business looks good, Sam," he said. "You're full up."

Sam's enthusiasm evaporated. He pulled a long face.

"Loss leaders. We give discounts so the rooms won't stay empty."

Hecky didn't try to hide his disbelief.

"To tell you the truth," Sam said confidentially, "we're not even holding our own. The upkeep! Which comes to what I want to mention."

"The five hundred. I already accepted, Sam. I don't need the song and dance."

Sam drank some Scotch, smacking his lips. "Two-fifty," he said.

Hecky stared at him, gripping the armrests.

"You promised five," he said slowly.

"I was hoping five." Sam dug his elbows into his stomach, palms-up. "I figured to steal a little from the band, from the dance team, make it up that way." He shook his head. "You know the union—they could shut me down."

"You knew that when you said five."

Sam didn't deny it. "I was still hoping."

"A year ago I played here for how much?" Hecky asked, rising from his chair. "All right, today is not a year ago. But I'm still Hecky Brown. Don't you forget that." He put his face close to Sam's. "You don't pay two-fifty for Hecky Brown!"

"Maybe three hundred," Sam conceded, wringing his hands. "Out of my own pocket."

"I piss on your three hundred!"

Sam said calmly, "Don't be foolish. Face facts, there's a cloud over your head. Who else is offering that much?"

It was true. No one else was offering anything. He was a pariah all over the state of New York.

"If it was up to me personally," Sam went on, "I'd pay you the moon. But business is business. Now, you drove all the way up here. You want to go home empty? Take the two-fifty."

Sam had Hecky over a barrel and they all knew it.

Hecky whispered, "You said three hundred."

"I'll see what I can do."

Sam glanced at his gold watch. Then he set his glass aside and patted Hecky on the shoulder.

"Break your own rule. Have a drink. You'll feel better."

Sam wanted everybody at the Catskill Manor to feel good, even when they were being cheated.

He smiled encouragingly and walked out of the room.

Neither Howard nor Hecky said anything. Howard walked to the liquor cabinet and filled one of Sam's stemmed glasses half-full of good Scotch. He offered it to his friend. Hecky stared at the glass for a moment, then took it, and tossed off the whisky neat.

Fourteen

Hecky dominated his table in the bar. Surrounded by admirers, his big bow tie hanging loose, his shirt unbuttoned, he continued to joke, goosing girls, signing autographs with a flourish. He told dirty stories loud enough for everyone to hear, and the bar resounded with laughter. He drank Scotch after Scotch, his broad, sweaty face twisted into a perpetual grin. His glowering eyes went unnoticed by the crowd.

But Howard noticed. He sat at the bar, next to a tall blonde with a fox stole draped about her soft, bare shoulders. She laughed at everything Hecky said, and Howard joined her in laughter, although he knew that Hecky's mood was anything but humorous.

"Isn't he fantastic?" the blonde said, crossing her legs. "I could watch him every night. He's so hilarious." Languorously, she looked Howard over. "You a guest here?"

Howard nodded and sipped his drink. This time he was going to play hard to get.

"What do you do?"

"I'm a dentist," he said.

"Professionally?"

He nodded again. Was there any other kind of dentist?

She smiled and offered her hand, bent daintily at the wrist. "I'm Sandy."

"Herman," Howard said, taking her hand. "Herman Miller."

"You have your own practice?"

"Yes, but I may have to take in a partner." Howard put on his concerned expression. "It's getting too big for one man."

"Are you by any chance . . ." Sandy paused, demurely lowering her eyes, ". . . attached?"

"Only to my work."

Sandy's smile broadened. She moved closer to Howard until their knees touched.

Sam appeared in the doorway, wearing an almost iridescent-green dinner jacket. He waited until Hecky had seen him, then came forward with outstretched arms. He carried an envelope in one hand.

"What can I say?" Sam enthused. "I'm speechless; words fail me. One of the great performances!"

He leaned over and kissed Hecky on top of the head. At the same time, he slipped the envelope into Hecky's pocket.

"You can tell your children," Sam said to the girls at Hecky's table, "and your grandchildren you saw one of the all-time greats—without peer!"

As Sam talked, Hecky took out the envelope, counting the money inside. Then he counted it again. He still couldn't believe it.

"Two-fifty?" Hecky said. After such a performance?

"I did what I could. But maybe next month . . ."

"You said three hundred."

"By popular demand . . ."

"Out of your own pocket?"

Hecky rose slowly to his feet. Sam's promoter's grin remained rigidly in place as Hecky grasped the lapels of his jacket and began to shake him.

"Show me your pockets," Hecky demanded in an outraged, drunken voice.

Sam's sunglasses slid down his nose. He tried to pull Hecky's hands away.

"What's inside there?" Hecky asked, sticking a hand into Sam's pocket. "Show me. What comes out of your pockets? Sympathy? Appreciation?"

The laughter and the talk suddenly stopped. Everyone waited to see if Hecky was still joking.

"Leave me go," Sam stammered.

"Blood comes out!"

Hecky delved into Sam's other pocket, dumping loose change, keys, and credit cards onto the floor. Sam glanced around for help, his face pale beneath the artificial tan.

"You *vonce!*" Hecky cursed him in Yiddish. "You nothing! Promises."

A girl screamed, the others backed away from the table. Two waiters rushed forward, grabbing Hecky's arms. He began to struggle.

"Liar!" Hecky shrieked.

"Get him out of here," Sam said to the waiters. "Out!"

"Lick my shoes!"

"Drop dead!"

Several people were shouting now. Hecky shook the waiters off. He stood in the middle of the barroom floor, trembling with rage. The envelope containing the two hundred and fifty dollars lay abandoned under the table.

Howard stepped between Hecky and Sam. He put his hand gently on his friend's shoulder and tried to lead him toward the door.

"Come on, Hecky . . ." he began but Hecky pushed him away.

"It's Howard, your friend."

"You're not my friend," Hecky said and lunged toward Sam again.

This time the waiters grabbed him and dragged him toward the door. "I'm Hecky Brown!" he shouted but they held onto him. He managed to make one obscene gesture toward Sam—a forcefully raised middle finger—before he was dragged out.

"You'll crawl in the gutter!" Sam called after him. "Commie son-of-a-bitch!"

Howard retrieved the envelope from beneath the table. Then he followed Hecky out to the parking lot.

Fifteen

On the way home Howard drove again. Hecky sat
slumped in the seat beside him, his face turned toward
the window. Their bags had been thrown into the back
of the Studebaker, their jackets tossed on top of the
bags. The excitement Howard had felt on the trip up
was gone now. He shared Hecky's depression.

He took out the envelope and pushed it toward
Hecky. "I found it on the floor."

Hecky looked at the envelope. For a moment he
didn't seem to recognize it. Then he took it and stuffed
it into his pocket. He rested his head against the seat
and closed his eyes.

Howard drove on through the darkness. Neither of
them spoke.

It was very late when Howard pulled up in front
of Hecky's apartment house on Central Park West.
Hecky hadn't changed his position, but his eyes were

open and he stared out at the deserted pavement as if it were a strange and forbidding neighborhood.

"You're home, Hecky."

But Hecky didn't move.

"All you need is a little sleep," Howard said encouragingly.

Hecky shook his head, without speaking.

"Money's money," Howard added. "Two-fifty is still two-fifty. It buys groceries."

It was no use. After such a night. Hecky couldn't face his family.

"You needed the money. Your wife will understand."

"I can't." Hecky's voice was no more than a whisper. "I can't."

Howard started the car and drove through Central Park. Hecky could sleep at his place and go home in the morning.

He parked in front of the building, next to a fire hydrant. The doorman could move the car in the morning—Howard was too tired to search for another spot. He and Hecky carried the bags up together, dragging their heels all the way.

Howard welcomed Hecky into his new apartment with a grand gesture.

"You can sleep on the couch," Howard said. "It's very comfortable." He fluffed up the pillows. "Brand-new, see?"

Hecky sat down on the sofa, folding his hands. He didn't seem to know where he was.

"You want some coffee?"

Hecky didn't answer. When he finally spoke, what he said had nothing to do with Howard's question.

"It's all Brownstein's fault. I wouldn't be in trouble if it wasn't for Brownstein."

"Who?"

"Brownstein," Hecky repeated. "Hershell Brownstein."

"Who's Hershell Brownstein?"

Hecky didn't hear. He was thinking about the insults he had received that night and the degradation of the blacklist. There had been a time when Hecky would have walked out of the Catskill Manor rather than perform for only three hundred dollars. And there had been a time when Hecky would have told Francis X. Hennessy to go to hell.

"You can't make a deal with Brownstein," he said. "That's the trouble. He won't listen to reason. You have to kill him."

Hecky stood up and walked slowly to the window. Howard watched him carefully.

"Is that your real name?" Howard asked. "Hershell Brownstein?"

Hecky nodded. "If only he would leave me alone, I could do it then. But he won't play ball. To him, it's all black and white. Some things you do; some things you don't do." He opened a window. "He thinks he's back on the street."

Howard moved toward Hecky, who was leaning out the open window, his hands on the sill. Howard was afraid he would try to jump.

"Brownstein, lay off!" Hecky shouted into the night. "You hear me? Lay off or I'll kill you!"

Howard gently took his arm. "People change their names, it's no crime."

"What do you know? Who the hell are you, a newcomer?"

"Why don't you sit down?" Howard said, leading him back toward the couch.

"Why don't you shut up?" Hecky jerked his arm

away. "You think you're so special. Talent is no protection. You do what they say, or else!"

"Would you like some tea?" Howard wished he would calm down.

"You've got a nice apartment," Hecky said, looking around. "Very nice."

"Thank you."

As Hecky prowled around the apartment, inspecting it, Howard closed the window with studied casualness.

"You've got nice things," Hecky said. "Hi-fi, TV, nice furniture. You like this apartment, I bet."

Howard nodded. He didn't like the stern tone of Hecky's voice or his aggressive manner. Hecky was playing another role, one Howard had never seen before.

"You worked hard for it; you deserve it. You want to keep it, right?"

"Cocoa?"

"I asked you a question."

"Sure I want to keep it."

"Then I suggest you answer the question." It was the voice of Francis X. Hennessy. "With sincerity. Sincerity is the key."

"Maybe you should call your wife," Howard suggested, trying to ignore the outbursts. "Let her at least know where you are."

"Where did you go last week?" Hecky demanded.

"Nowhere."

"Nowhere is somewhere. From the heart, please. No credit unless it comes from the heart."

"Here and there. Round and about. What can I say?"

"Where did you go last year?" Hecky advanced, jabbing the air with his finger. "The year before? Who did you see? Where did you march? What did you sign?"

"Nothing."

Suddenly Howard realized Hecky was imitating the man who had blacklisted him. It made Howard nervous.

"That girl you go with," Hecky continued, "the one from the show, what's her name?"

"Florence?"

"A troublemaker. I heard how she talked on the set. Subversive—a Red. You liked that girl?"

"I like her," Howard admitted. He was backed against the arm of the sofa.

"What's her name?"

"I told you."

"Her full name!"

"Florence Barrett." Howard fell backwards onto the cushions.

"You know she's a Red?"

"Cut it out, Hecky. I don't like this game."

"Game?" Hecky laughed hollowly. "You call this a game? This is no game, Mr. Prince. We are up against a ruthless enemy who you might be helping, aiding, abetting. You want all this, your fame and fortune . . ."

"What do you want me to say?"

"In your own words," Hecky said.

"Sure I do. It's mine."

"Who says?"

"I paid for it!"

"You think that matters?"

Howard got up and moved toward the dining room. Hecky followed relentlessly.

"This is my place," Howard said. He was defensive,

angry. "I didn't steal it. I didn't hurt anybody to get it."

"Who cares?"

"*I* care!" Howard felt he was trapped in a crazy world between Florence's idealism and the fanaticism of the people Hecky was portraying.

"Who are you?" Hecky snarled, pushing his face close to Howard's. "You think you're somebody? You think because you're paid, you're entitled? We'll blow you out like a match." He blew in Howard's face. "Answer the question!"

"What question?"

"The girl."

"I don't know." Howard was almost whispering.

"You can find out." What does she say to you? At night, in bed, when she thinks she's safe . . ."

Hecky paused, and smiled a thin smile. His voice became soft, sympathetic. "You're in love—two nice young people. She trusts you . . ."

"We broke up," Howard blurted out, unable to stand the interrogation any longer. "I don't see her anymore. I don't know anything. Stop it!"

Hecky's eyes clouded over. The persona of Francis X. Hennessy slipped away.

"Cut it out. I've had enough, Hecky." He pointed to the couch. "Lie down or go home."

But Hecky stayed where he was. He closed his eyes, clinging to one of the dining-room chairs.

"He's got me by the throat," he moaned, not acting any longer. "He'll never let go, that one. Squeezing, squeezing . . . I can't breathe."

Howard watched, horrified. Hecky was defenseless, alone, his career ruined. There was nothing Howard, or anyone else, could do.

"Double double," Hecky chanted, "Brown's in trouble. No way out, they broke his bubble. You didn't know I was a poet. . . . I read someplace, a fox caught in a trap, he'll bite off his own leg to get out. A leg, that's easy. . . ." He began to talk faster. "He won't settle for a leg. He won't compromise. He won't live and let live. But he won't die!"

Hecky was in anguish. He rocked back and forth on the balls of his feet, crying to himself.

"Brownstein, you villain, I hate you so. Why won't you die?"

Howard took Hecky's hand and led him to the couch. He stretched out without protest this time. Howard pulled off his shoes, slipped a pillow beneath his head, and went for a blanket in the bedroom, which he spread over Hecky's bulky form.

"Try to sleep," Howard said. "You'll feel better in the morning."

Hecky didn't answer. He kept his eyes clamped shut, his face twisted by pain and sorrow.

Howard left him. He switched off the lights and went into the bedroom. He took off his own shoes, fell backwards across the bed, and was immediately asleep.

Hecky did not sleep. He lay in the darkness, staring at the reflection of the street lights on the ceiling. He had only one chance left, and he would take it, even though it meant going against everything he had ever believed in.

He threw the blanket aside and sat up. He crossed the room to Howard's desk and switched on the reading lamp. He took down Howard's books and examined them. Some were written by Russian authors, which would please Hennessy.

Hecky opened the desk drawers. He took out a new script and thumbed through it. He unfolded letters, spread them out on the desk top, and began to read.

Being a spy was easy.

Sixteen

Phil Sussman's elegant Fifth Avenue apartment was
filled with the right people. They stood about in small
groups, talking with the easy animation of the rich
and the well-connected. Network executives mixed
with critics, producers, actors, agents, and important
sponsors. The waiter moved with difficulty among the
groups, balancing a tray of drinks. He was followed
by a maid in a starched white uniform, carrying
another tray loaded with canapés. The party was in
celebration of "Grand Central," the season's most successful television series.

Sussman stood in a corner, his back to his Picasso
engraving, chatting with a middle-aged couple. The
man was a Wall Street seer; his wife was well-coifed
and decorated with cameos.

"You must be so excited," the woman was saying,
"the show going from a half-hour to an hour."

"I was expecting it. With those ratings . . ." Sussman
paused to watch a particularly beautiful actress navi-

gate the room, her gold lame gown clinging to her many curves. She leaned on the piano, where a black man in a tuxedo sat, playing a lively version of "Love for Sale."

"They're not fools upstairs," Sussman went on, referring to the men who ran the network. "They know what they've got."

"Do you think you can get the same quality in an hour?" the man asked.

"One thing I've learned in this business—when you've got the talent, you've got the quality."

The three of them turned in unison and looked across the room, at Howard. Several people were clustered about him, listening eagerly to everything he said. He was the only writer present, a tribute to his importance. He wore a tuxedo for the first time in his life, and he liked the feel of it.

"Actually," Howard said, in response to a question from one of the admirers, "you could say modern American writing began with *Huckleberry Finn*. If that's what you want to say."

A young woman stepped forward, dragging her date by the hand. "What about Melville? Especially today . . ." She gasped. "The sense of evil . . ."

Howard readily agreed. "How can you leave out Melville?"

"Do you think television is closer to literature or drama?"

Howard compromised. "I'd say in the middle."

"But is it really an art form?" the young man asked.

"What is art? For that matter, what is form? A bird flies . . ." Howard passed his open hand through the air, winging it. "Does he know the answer? Does he even know the question?"

His audience nodded appreciatively.

Sussman left the older couple and joined Howard's group. Howard was the star, after all. He was followed by Tom Hampton, who was steering another man by the elbow. The man had bushy eyebrows combed upward and a double chin that draped over the edge of his collar. Sussman knew he must be a sponsor or Tom Hampton wouldn't be escorting him around.

"Phil . . . Howard . . ." Hampton said loudly. "I want you to meet Hubert Jackson—Jackson Supermarkets. You know, out on the Island?"

The three of them shook hands. Howard was afraid Hubert Jackson would crush his fingers.

"Congratulations, gentlemen," Jackson said.

"Hubert's a great fan of your show," Hampton told them.

"Never miss it." Jackson made it sound like a duty.

"But he's a little concerned about some of the actors you've been using."

Sussman assured him, "We go for the best, Mr. Jackson."

"Well, in my opinion, some of them are pretty pink, Mr. Sussman."

"That's the makeup," said Howard.

Hampton quickly countered. "I told Hubert we're as concerned as he is. Not that they are, of course . . . the actors . . ." He nervously stroked his salt-and-pepper mustache. "We take every precaution."

Sussman agreed. "The slightest hint."

"Well, I know my customers," Jackson said. "They think a company's sponsoring Reds, they just won't buy that brand."

"How do they know?" Howard asked, smiling.

"I tell them. Put a sign right up above the product."

"I thought you might send Hubert a list of actors

you plan to use," Hampton said to Sussman. "Let him look them over and give you any ideas he has."

"Absolutely."

"You'll get full cooperation from us, Hubert." Hampton took Jackson's arm again. "Nothing to worry about. Thanks, boys."

He gave Howard a dirty look and led Jackson away.

"How many stores has he got?" Howard asked.

"Three, maybe four," Sussman said.

"He's only got three stores and he tells a whole network who to hire?" Howard couldn't believe it.

Sussman shrugged. "Who wants trouble?" He preferred not to think about it and excused himself.

The actress in the gold lamé gown left the piano. Howard saw her whispering with her agent, a garrulous, amusing Californian named Jerry, and glancing at him. The time had come for Jerry and his client to move in on "Grand Central."

"Ellen just signed up with us, Howard," Jerry said, bringing her over. "And we're looking for someone to create a series for her."

Ellen showed Howard a perfect set of teeth.

"She's one of those rarities in our business, Howard. She's beautiful and a great actress."

"Not in front of me, Jerry," Ellen said.

"You're our first choice," Jerry confided. "Howard, we need a writer, not a hack."

Ellen batted long, black lashes. "I'm sure Howard's too busy."

"No, listen," Howard said gallantly, "I'm always ready to talk."

When Howard left his apartment building the next morning, walking across town to the First National

City Bank, he was followed by a well-dressed man in a raincoat. While Howard cashed two checks for scripts he had submitted, the man waited outside the windows of Abercrombie's, pretending to study the display of hunting clothes.

Howard emerged from the bank in high spirits. He hailed a taxi, telling the driver to take him to Greenberg's Dairy Restaurant, on Bleecker Street, never noticing the cab that followed his all the way down Fifth Avenue.

The others were expecting him. Alfred, Delany, and Phelps sat at the table in the back, anxious to be paid for their scripts. Howard hurriedly placed his order for scrambled eggs, then sat down.

He casually pulled two personal checks from his pocket. "Your check, Herb," he said, handing it over in a lordly manner. "Yours, Bill. Here you go. Yours didn't come yet, Allie. You were late with the script, remember?" He shook a finger at Alfred. "Got to watch that."

Alfred scowled at him, but didn't say anything.

"Here's your script back," Howard said to Phelps, handing him a manila envelope. "Needs a rewrite, I'm afraid."

Phelps was surprised. "What didn't Sussman like?"

"Didn't give it to him." Howard gazed around the restaurant, wondering if any of the customers recognized him as the famous television writer.

"What do you mean," Alfred whispered, "you didn't give it to him?"

"Wasn't ready."

Alfred was flabbergasted.

"Allie," Howard patiently explained, "you don't expect me to hand in just anything. I've got a reputation. My name's going on that script."

Alfred clenched his fists. *"Howard . . ."* he warned.

Phelps headed Alfred off. "I'll try to write up to your standards, Howard."

"You sure going to an hour isn't too much pressure?" Howard asked.

The others looked at one another. They would just have to humor him.

"The stories seem a little thin lately," he added. "The key is *substance*. I've been reading the Eugene O'Neill plays and I'd like something more along those lines."

"Only with more laughs," said Alfred.

"But gutsy." Howard was oblivious to the sarcasm. "Also, I made a deal for a new series."

"We got our hands full with this one."

"You'll just have to get more writers." Howard had already promised Ellen he'd get cracking. "Right now, what I need is a pilot script."

"How about Eugene O'Neill?" Delany suggested.

"He's dead, Herb." Howard was proud of his insider's knowledge.

"What's the subject?"

"Woman reporter. Great idea, isn't it? Got the perfect actress for the lead. With her and a Howard Prince script . . ." Howard snapped his fingers.

"We'll look around for somebody," Phelps promised.

"But *good,* Bill." Howard leaned earnestly across the table. "Remember, blacklisted isn't enough."

Alfred jumped to his feet. He was about to punch Howard in the mouth when the waiter arrived.

"Scrambled eggs, loose," the waiter chanted, sliding the plate across. "Whitefish. Eggplant roast. Soybean casserole. Eat in good health."

Alfred sat down again. The four of them ate in silence.

No one noticed the well-dressed man in a raincoat who had entered the restaurant a few minutes before, taking a table by the door.

Seventeen

Howard sat in his new apartment for days, waiting for Florence to call. He had sent her a check to help cover expenses for her pamphlet, "Facts About Blacklist," hoping that would lead to their reconciliation. He had taken a considerable risk by sending her the money, but Florence didn't respond.

When the telephone finally did ring, it was only Alfred. He couldn't find a writer for Howard's new television series.

"What are you talking about?" Howard said irritably. "You can't find a writer? I just need a script, not the Ten Commandments. . . ."

Alfred explained that there were no good writers available.

"Allie, a writer's a writer. They're all over the place."

Alfred, controlling his anger, explained that good writers and hacks were not the same thing.

"Allie, this is Howard." Maybe Alfred had forgotten that Howard was a pro—*the* pro. "I've been around this business. I know how it's done. . . ."

If Howard knew so much about it, Alfred shouted, then he could write the pilot script himself.

"All right," Howard shouted back, "I will!"

They slammed the phone down simultaneously.

Howard flipped open the telephone book to the Yellow Pages, running his finger down the list of typewriter suppliers. He was Howard Prince, the famous writer, and all he needed to prove it was a typewriter.

He ordered an electric one. It would allow him to write scripts much faster than a manual typewriter. Time was very important to Howard Prince.

The electric typewriter arrived that afternoon. Howard set it on his desk and, around it, arranged freshly sharpened pencils, typing paper, carbons, and correction fluid. Then he got a fresh cup of coffee and sat down to confront the machine.

He plugged it in, but didn't touch the keyboard. It was more complicated than he had expected. Howard had seen plenty of typewriters but had never actually used one—not an electric one, anyway. All those buttons and switches were intimidating.

He sipped his coffee. Finally, he slipped a sheet of paper into the roller and punched a key. Nothing happened. The machine hadn't been turned on. He flipped the switch and a red light glowed; the typewriter began to hum. He raised one finger and brought it down on the keyboard.

With a high-pitched shriek, the carriage leapt to one side. Howard was so surprised he almost turned his chair over backwards. He wiped the spilled coffee from his trousers, and returned the carriage to its starting position.

Cautiously, he began to type. This time the letters struck the paper, as they were intended to do, but he mistakenly touched several keys at one time, getting them tangled. He pulled them apart, getting ink on his fingers, he wiped it off on his handkerchief, and replaced the sheet of paper. Now he was really ready.

But the words wouldn't come. He stared at the white paper, and it stared back. Once he raised his hands, but they fell back into his lap, and stayed there.

The telephone rang. Howard quickly grabbed the receiver.

"Hello, hello . . ." he said gratefully.

It was Meyer, not Florence. But at least it was somebody.

"Oh, hi, Meyer . . . just working, that's all. . . . No, really, you're not disturbing me. I can use a break."

Meyer wanted to know if Howard could get him two tickets for the network quiz show.

"Of course, certainly. I'll call the producer; he's a friend of mine." Howard let that soak in. "I'll get you house seats."

Meyer thanked him, a new note of respect in his voice.

"Meyer, it's no trouble. A phone call." Howard liked his brother, in spite of their differences. "Give my regards."

He hung up and returned to the typewriter. But still the words wouldn't come. He began to pace the floor, the way writers were supposed to do. It didn't help. He sat down again, flooded with a sense of loneliness. Writing was no fun. He missed his old job cashiering at the Friendly Tavern, the contact with people. The notebook that Margo had given him lay on the desk, as a reminder.

He snatched up the telephone and dialed a familiar number.

"Danny," he said happily, "you want to get down on the Dodgers?"

Danny did want to get down. Howard flipped open the notebook and began to scribble.

"Two-and-a-half." Those were the odds. "Fifty, right. . . ." He felt better already.

Danny was about to hang up.

"Hey," Howard said, "how's business? You don't say. I'm certainly glad to hear that. I mean, people ought to eat more fruit. It's healthy. . . ."

Making conversation with Danny wasn't easy. He said he had to get back to work.

"Sure, Danny, I know you're busy. See you."

Reluctantly, Howard hung up. Everybody was busy. Nobody had time for Howie anymore.

On an impulse, he grabbed his jacket and left the apartment.

Howard knew he was being followed as soon as he stepped off the elevator. A man in a raincoat stood on the pavement outside the lobby, turning his back as Howard came out. Howard had seen him lurking on the street the day before, and he also thought he had seen him as he was leaving Greenberg's Dairy Restaurant.

Howard waited until he reached the corner of Lexington Avenue, then quickly looked back. There the man was, less than one hundred yards behind him. Howard felt a cold chill and began to walk faster.

He was heading for Brentano's where Florence worked. Howard had kept up with her through friends at the network, had passed the bookstore several times, thinking he might meet her accidentally outside, but had never gone in. He wasn't going to demean himself.

This time he walked directly into the store. It was lunch hour and the aisles were crowded with people silently thumbing through books or gazing up at the shelves. The whisper of turning pages and an occasional mumbled conversation gave Howard the creeps.

He spotted Florence near the rear of the store, talking to a woman in a feathered hat. He thought she had seen him, but she ignored him. He walked over and stood with hands on hips, waiting for her to finish with the customer.

Florence wore the same low-cut dress she had on the day they visited the Cloisters together. Her black hair was gathered in a scarf. Howard felt more than a twinge of regret—she really was beautiful.

Finally, the woman picked up her book and left.

"Listen," Howard said, trying to be forceful, "this is ridiculous. I decided we should get back together again."

Florence looked at Howard disinterestedly. "Really?"

"You don't have to actually move in," he conceded. "My place, your place . . . wherever we are, that's where we are."

"I'm not interested in just a bed partner."

Florence began to arrange books on the shelves, making a show of ignoring him.

"I'm talking as a writer." Howard really believed what he was saying. "A writer needs someone to bounce ideas off . . . someone he respects, to inspire him."

"I'm flattered," she said with heavy sarcasm.

"Well, it's a compliment."

"But I think all you want is a female body, someone warm and willing, who won't make demands."

"I won't make demands either," he promised. "We'll be even."

"I insist on demands."

"Then I'll make demands!"

He was almost shouting. He looked behind him and saw the man in the raincoat perusing the shelves. He seemed to be interested in spy stories.

"Why are you so nervous?" Florence asked.

"I'm not nervous. I just want to renew our relationship." Howard decided to be reasonable. "Florence, I know how you feel. I respect you for it, believe me. You want to be Joan of Arc . . ."

"Interesting, that's how you see me. Burned at the stake."

Florence walked away, Howard following.

"Everything is not hostility," he whispered. "You think I like the blacklist? I hate the blacklist! Didn't I send you money for the pamphlet?"

Florence wasn't impressed. Money was not a commitment.

"What can I do?" Howard asked. "It's the network, the sponsors. It's the *government*. They'd wipe me out."

Florence turned to face him. "You're a creative person. They can't stop you from writing."

"They won't put it on the air."

"You could write plays . . . novels . . ."

"Who'd publish them?" There was no escape— even if Howard *could* write plays and novels. "They blacklist you there, too."

"Poetry."

Poetry would not pay for Howard's new apartment, his furniture, his clothes. If only she would give up a little idealism . . .

"And live on what?" Howard asked. "Air? Some crummy job? Work a cash register someplace?"

"If a job is honest, if you can go home when it's over, and face yourself . . ."

"Come home and face me," he pleaded.

". . . and then go out and fight for what you believe."

"Why do you always want to fight? Once and for all, I'm not looking for trouble."

"A writer looks for trouble," she said defiantly. "And it only takes one man to say no—just one."

Howard didn't have the courage to be that one man. He didn't have the desire, either.

"Why did I come here?" he asked. "I should have my head examined. I come to take you back and you're looking to get me killed, just because I rejected you."

"*You* rejected *me?*"

"But I'm willing to forget that," he quickly added.

"I'm the one who walked out, remember?"

"What else could you do?" Howard was hurt. "It was my apartment."

Several customers stood watching the argument. The silence was potent.

"Fine, Howard," Florence said, speaking through clenched teeth. "If that's what you need for your manhood, you rejected me. I hope it makes you very happy."

This time she walked away too fast for Howard to follow.

He picked up a heavy volume and considered throwing it at her. Then he noticed that the man in the raincoat was watching him.

Howard replaced the book and stomped out of the store.

Eighteen

Rain clouds threatened as Howard stepped out of a cab in front of the studio. He paid the driver and glanced back up Forty-second Street. Another cab had turned the corner from Broadway, just as Howard's had, and it pulled up to the curb a block away. No one got out, but Howard knew a man in a raincoat was sitting in the backseat, watching him.

He hurried into the building, ignoring the smiles and nods of the network employees. Being famous was not as much fun as it used to be.

He took the elevator to the sixth floor, walking directly to Sussman's office. Sussman had called him in, Howard suspected, for a last-minute script conference, and he looked forward to the usual congratulations. He had come to expect flattery.

Sussman smiled when he saw Howard, pointing to a chair. But, instead of praising the latest script, he started talking about a subpoena.

"A subpoena? For me?"

Sussman nodded but didn't look at him. "To appear before the House Un-American Committee."

"When?" Howard felt sick. "How do you know?"

"They found out upstairs. It hasn't been issued yet, but any minute."

"But I'm not a Communist."

"Howard, you've got to go," Sussman said emphatically. "I don't like it anymore than you do. But, if you don't do it, you don't work."

Howard couldn't believe that this was happening to him. He was no lefto. All he wanted was money, girls, fame. What could be more American?

Sussman was afraid he would lose his best writer. Exasperated, he threw his pen down on the desk. "Why don't they just go away and let us do the show? Who needs this?"

Howard seized on Sussman's frustration. "You know, Phil, I never believed what Florence said about you."

"Crazy broad . . ." Sussman felt that Florence had deserted him and the show.

"I saw how hard it was for you to fire Hecky," Howard went on.

"I had a migraine for a week."

Howard got up and began to pace up and down Sussman's office. "It just takes one guy to say no to them—just one."

"What can I do, Howard?"

Howard paused and said, "You can be that guy."

Sussman frowned, then a faraway look came into his eyes. The idea obviously appealed to him.

"I'm serious," Howard said, urging him on. "If one person says no, especially a guy like you. You're respected; you're a big name. Tell them no."

Howard could tell that Sussman was wavering.

"Who the hell are they, anyway?" Howard asked. "Come on, Phil. Take a stand—the real you." Howard was counting on Sussman to save him from the Committee.

Sussman swallowed. He picked up the telephone and told his secretary, "Get me Hampton."

While Sussman waited, he stared straight ahead, his jaw set—the picture of determination. Howard knew Florence would be proud of them for what they were about to do.

"Hello, Tom? . . . Phil, here. There's no reason Howard Prince has to go to that Committee . . ."

His voice was tough and self-assured.

"That's right," he added. "It's our network. Who the hell are they, giving us orders? . . . No, you listen to me. He doesn't *have* to go. What are we, sheep? We make a stand. Tell them to get off his back, stop threatening, piss off, or *they're* in trouble." He thumped the desk with his fist. "We fight, Tom. We show them there's some people they can't scare. We tell them flat-out—Howard Prince doesn't go!"

Sussman listened to Hampton for a while. He nodded, his militant expression unchanged, and then he hung up.

"Well," he said to Howard, "you got to testify."

They had been summoned to the top floor of the network building. Howard and Sussman rode up in the elevator together, in silence. Howard was scared. He knew that if he wanted to take care of Number One, he would have to cooperate.

Sussman led him through the carpeted foyer into the network's paneled boardroom. Several men sat in a semi-circle around a chair reserved for Howard. Tom Hampton waved him toward the hot seat. Next to him sat Francis X. Hennessy, wearing a dark suit, his crew cut well-brushed. And next to Hennessy sat the man in the raincoat who had been following Howard. He seemed less sinister at close range, but Howard felt threatened being in the same room with a spy.

The network's lawyer adjusted his spectacles, opened his black briefcase, and took out a sheet of paper. In a smooth, professional manner he began to explain that Howard was in trouble. Investigators for the Freedom Information Service had collected damaging evidence against Howard, and he would have to testify before the House Committee on Un-American Activities if he wanted to continue working. He said that many of Howard's friends were Communists or Communist dupes. Did Howard know, for instance, that Alfred Miller was a Communist sympathizer?

Howard lied; he said he didn't know that.

The lawyer was pleased. "That's exactly what you'll tell the Committee."

"He's a friend of mine," Howard added, trying to sound casual. "Allie Miller, we went to school together."

"You had no idea he was a Communist?"

"He was only twelve."

No one was amused.

"You have no idea *now?*" the lawyer asked.

"We don't talk about politics."

"And the other men . . ." The lawyer consulted his papers. "Delany and Phelps?"

"Friends of Allie's."

"And the girl, Florence Barrett?"

"Oh," Howard said dismissively, "that was only sex."

Hennessy leaned forward. "Is that why you gave money to her pro-Communist publication?"

Howard wondered how he knew about that. What else did they know?

"She wanted to start a magazine," he said. "I was dating her. Who knew what kind?"

Hampton asked the lawyer, "Will that satisfy the Committee?"

"He's cooperating. We'll write him a strong anti-Communist statement to go with his testimony. That ought to do it."

"Why do I have to go at all?" Howard asked.

No one paid him any attention.

"Does it have to be open to the public?" Hampton wanted to know. "Won't they consent to an executive session? We don't need the publicity."

The lawyer said dryly, "They do. I think they can be persuaded, though, since he's being cooperative."

"Can't we fix somebody?" Howard asked. "It doesn't cost much. They're only Congressmen."

"Nothing to worry about, Howard," Hampton assured him. "They'll be posing for pictures with you."

"All they want is a friendly witness," the lawyer said.

The men in the room smiled. Howard felt a cold chill down his back.

Nineteen

Alfred was hospitalized with a ruptured ulcer, but Howard didn't hear about it until the following day when Bill Phelps telephoned him from Mount Sinai Hospital. Howard took a cab straight down, finding a very pale Alfred propped up in bed, a needle in one arm with a rubber tube attached to a bottle of clear liquid suspended above him. Phelps and Herb Delany stood awkwardly next to the bed, wishing they could do something to help. There were no flowers in the room.

"Hi, Howard," Alfred said weakly.

"Gee," said Howard, forgiving Alfred for not finding him a writer for his new series, "you gotta lay off health foods. Why don't they operate? Get rid of that ulcer already."

"Then how would I know when I'm angry?"

"Nobody knows how to relax anymore," Howard complained, although he was as nervous as everyone else. "You gotta ride with the punches."

Alfred knew he was bluffing. "What about the subpoena?" The news was already out.

"Nothing, it's fine." Howard didn't want to talk about it. "Relax."

"They write the statement for you?"

Howard nodded. "I'd let you read it, only you'd start bleeding again."

Alfred and the others exchanged glances.

"Allie," Howard said, "don't worry. Take care of yourself. Worry about who'll write the scripts while you're in here."

"We've got a very good writer," Delany told him. "You won't be ashamed."

"Blacklisted?" That was proof of quality.

"Impeccably. Named by his own brother-in-law."

A nurse brought in a glass of milk for Alfred. She looked at his visitors with stern disapproval.

"Visiting hours are over," she announced.

"I'm Dr. Prince."

The nurse looked skeptically at Howard.

"Consultation," he added.

She turned to Phelps and Delany.

"My associates," Howard said.

"Uh-huh." But she smiled as she went out.

Alfred drank some of the milk, then asked, "Howard, why do you think they want you to testify?"

"I'm a feather in their cap, Howard Prince. I'm a big writer."

"But why do they want you to give names? They already have our names. Why do they need you to tell them again?"

"All right," Howard admitted, "so it makes them look good. So what?"

Phelps and Delany looked away but Alfred said, "They don't care about names. They care about getting people to *give* names. They want to show there's nothing they can't get people to do."

Howard felt like a traitor. "I don't cooperate, you don't work. Nobody works. Is that what you guys want?"

"I think we're laying too much on him, Al," Phelps said. "Why should he take the rap?"

"I want him to know what he's doing."

"I'm helping!" Howard protested.

"You're helping them."

"I'm using them. I'm smarter than they are."

"Howard, the time for bullshit is over."

"Howard was insulted. "Who does it hurt if I'm friendly? Where is the personal crime? I tell them you're my friend, from public school. Am I hurting you more? They already got your name; you said so yourself."

"He's right," Phelps said. "They can't do any more to us. Why can't he just cooperate?"

"Tell them the truth?" Delany was against that.

"He won't have to. The network's made a deal. He says the Committee's great, they leave him alone."

"Everyone gets what he wants," Howard agreed. "Isn't that what it's all about?"

Alfred didn't answer.

"Allie, don't make a big thing. They only want the publicity."

"They want Howard Prince," Alfred said, "as an example, to scare people, to shut people up."

"I think he should take the Fifth," Delany decided.

"What's the Fifth?" Howard was confused.

"The Fifth Amendment. Your right not to incriminate yourself."

"Why should I take anything?" Howard asked. "It's all fixed."

"They might ask you some questions you don't want to answer," Delany explained. "But if you already answered one—like did you know Alfred—then you don't have the right anymore. Then you don't answer, they can cite you for contempt."

"But I'm going to answer."

"Schmuck!" Alfred said.

"I think he should go," Phelps said. "What the hell can he tell them?"

Delany disagreed. "I don't trust the Committee *or* the network. Take the Fifth."

"I don't want to take the Fifth!"

"You can't cooperate." Alfred made it sound like a crime.

"Don't be a loser all your life," Howard said. "Sometimes you have to compromise."

"Stop looking for an out."

The nurse opened the door to see what all the commotion was about. Howard grabbed the glass of milk and handed it to Alfred.

"You mustn't aggravate yourself," he said soothingly. "Drink your milk."

The nurse withdrew.

"You did a big favor, Howard," Alfred admitted, "for all of us. I don't have to tell you that."

"Who's asking?"

"You saved our ass." Alfred didn't want Howard to think he was ungrateful. "Don't you think I know that? You did what a friend does."

"I cooperate," Howard said, "your ass is still saved."

"You can't be on their side."

"Fine, I don't cooperate. I tell them they can shove it, right? Then you don't work, right?"

"I'll worry about that," Alfred told him.

"And where do I go? Back to the cash register,

right?" Howard experienced a moment of panic, realizing that Alfred wanted him to give everything up. "I don't believe this. You can't use your name, you're lying there bleeding, and you're telling me!"

"Al," Phelps said, "we can't ask him to do what he doesn't believe in."

"Protect yourself," Delany advised Howard. "Take the Fifth."

But Alfred shook his head emphatically.

"You always think there's a middle you can dance around in, Howard. I'm telling you, there's no middle here. And you can't lay this off on us. Whatever you do, you're doing it for yourself."

They stared at one another. Howard knew what Alfred said was true.

"You know who you sound like?" he asked, thinking of Florence. "A former friend of mine—another loser."

Howard picked up the glass again and handed it to Alfred.

"Drink your milk," he said bitterly.

Twenty

Howard was determined to write his own pilot script. He didn't need Alfred, Florence, Phelps, or Delany. He was Howard Prince, of "Grand Central" fame. He didn't need anybody.

He ordered a manual typewriter to replace the electric one. For a solid hour he sat in front of it, until he realized that manual typewriters didn't make writing television scripts any easier.

Suddenly, there was a knock on his door. Howard jumped up from his desk, then hesitated—he was afraid to answer. Once he would have welcomed the distraction; but now he didn't want unexpected callers.

Cautiously, he opened the door—and Hecky burst into the room.

"Nobody move!" he shouted. "This is a raid! Everybody out!"

Howard's heart skipped a beat. He thought it really was a raid, until he saw that Hecky was going through one of his famous acts. He stalked about the apartment, opening drawers, rummaging through books and magazines. He went into Howard's bedroom, emerging with his hands on his hips.

"We understand that you have a woman in your room," Hecky said officiously. "If not, why not?"

Howard grinned.

"Have you got one for me?" Hecky asked. "Have we met before?"

"You scared me."

"I was in the neighborhood and suddenly everything went black." He smiled sheepishly. "I'm disturbing you."

"Absolutely not."

"You really want to know," Hecky admitted, "I came to apologize for that terrible night. I wasn't myself."

Howard couldn't hold that against him. "Listen, you had a right."

"Two rights don't make a wrong. I gave you a very hard time. I'm sorry."

"Have a drink?"

"Before the sun is over the yardarm?" Hecky pretended to be shocked. "A small Scotch."

Howard went to the bar and took out his Haig and Haig Pinch. He poured them both a stiff drink, then went for ice cubes.

"How are things going?" he called from the kitchen.

"Not bad. Club dates out of town, but not bad— Scranton, Allentown. I'm very big in Pennsylvania. My wife found a job; the kids eat. We all got our health."

Howard brought him the drink. Hecky raised his glass in a toast.

"To a prince of a Prince," he said, and downed the Scotch. "I never learned to sip a drink. When I was little, every night before supper, my father would pour a one-shot glass full of whisky, say a prayer, and down it all went. I thought that was the way you drank."

Hecky set his glass on the coffee table, refusing a refill. "How's it going with you?"

"Fine." Howard decided not to mention the subpoena.

"I hear terrific. It's nice when nice happens to nice. It doesn't happen too often. You sure I'm not being a nuisance?"

"Positive."

"You know Johnny Parker, the actor?"

Howard remembered the name from a few years back.

"Blacklisted," Hecky said; the word made Howard wince. "He couldn't get arrested. Wife, three kids, you can imagine. Drove a cab for a while. Finally he gave it all up. He came from someplace out West—Oklahoma, Texas—out there someplace. Owned a little farm his father left him. Miserable." Hecky laughed. "He showed me pictures. You could go crazy there. But at least he could grow his own food, so he went back. We gave him a party; everybody cried. Six months later, right in the middle of his miserable property, they struck oil."

"You're kidding." That was the kind of story Howard liked to hear.

"Honest to God! Oil! Now he's a millionaire."

They laughed together for the first time in a long time.

"So you see," Hecky said, "every cloud has a silver lining."

"Have another drink."

"No, really. I came, I apologized; it's time to go."

Howard didn't want to be left alone. "Why don't we have dinner sometime?"

"I'd like that very much."

"Tonight?"

Hecky seemed suddenly bewildered and distant.

"Tonight," he said, "I'm busy."

"I'll give you a call."

"Don't call us; we'll call you." Hecky smiled. "If I had a dollar every time that was said to me . . . when I was first getting started, of course. Later on, I don't have to tell you, the shoe was on the other foot."

"I really will call." Howard meant it.

"I know you will. I was making a joke. You don't mind I came without phoning?"

"Of course not."

"Some people mind." Hecky shook Howard's hand. "You're a good person."

"I'll call you tomorrow," Howard promised. It was good to see Hecky on top of things again.

On his way out, Hecky paused and said, "Take care of yourself. The water is full of sharks."

Howard said good-bye and closed the door. He couldn't bring himself to sit down at the typewriter again.

He went to the window. Storm clouds were blowing in from Montauk and warm spring rain began to splatter the panes. It was the kind of afternoon to spend with a girl, quiet and intimate. Howard knew several girls he could invite over, but the one he wanted wouldn't come.

El Morocco was crowded. The tables near the stage were occupied mostly by celebrities and their friends, faces as familiar to the public as they were to the black-coated waiters scurrying among them with trays of drinks and champagne. The comedian performing on the stage was only part of the show—the patrons of El

Morocco spent as much time looking at one another as they spent watching the act.

The comedian was good, however, and the club resounded with laughter and applause. Few people remembered that the comedian's routines had been perfected by a different performer—Hecky Brown. The routines were still funny, the face was new, and that was all that mattered.

One person who did recognize the routines was Hecky himself. He sat alone at the bar, laughing and applauding with the others, knowing that the comedian would be paid ten times what Hecky was earning in the remote burgs of Pennsylvania, performing the same act. There was nothing he could do about it, so he laughed.

But there was resignation—a note of deep sadness—in Hecky's laughter. He looked around at the other customers. He recognized most of them, and a few he had once considered his friends. Now they all avoided him. He knew that even if his name were removed from the blacklist, he would never regain his place at the top. His reputation was ruined; he had lost the valuable momentum necessary to a successful performer.

He had not realized this fact until it was too late. He had betrayed Howard—and himself—spying for the Freedom Information Service. And it had made no real difference. He was still finished, washed up.

Hecky had been drinking since he left Howard's apartment. He couldn't afford the El Morocco, but tonight was a kind of celebration. He paid his bill when the act was over, tipping the bartender handsomely, and walked out slowly and with dignity.

Second Avenue was almost deserted. The rain had stopped and a fresh breeze blew across from Queens, where Hecky had grown up. He walked west, toward Central Park and the Plaza Hotel. In spite of the large amount of whisky he had consumed, he was not drunk. Hecky's euphoria was caused by something stronger than alcohol: he had stopped caring.

He checked into the Plaza, asking for a room with a view of the park. He also asked for a bottle of champagne. The bellhop led Hecky to an attractive, spacious room, switched on the lights, and drew back the curtains. Hecky tipped him five dollars.

When the man left, Hecky took off his jacket and hung it in a closet designed for large, expensive wardrobes. A moment later there was a knock at the door—another bellhop with champagne in a silver bucket. Hecky pressed a five-dollar bill into this man's hand.

He carefully unwound the wire around the neck of the bottle and applied his thumbs to the cork. It shot upward, releasing a bubbly torrent of wine. Hecky caught some in a glass, smiling appreciatively. Then he poured the glass full and turned to face the gilt-edged mirror in one corner of the room. He toasted himself grandly.

He refilled his glass and walked over to the bed. He tested its softness and found it very inviting. Sitting down on the edge, he drained the glass, and set it carefully on the bedside table. He took four vials of sleeping pills from his pocket—reds, yellows, greens, and blues—emptied them onto the table, and lined the pills up.

It was almost time now. He refilled his glass, and began to take the pills one at a time, sipping the vintage champagne after each one. He ran out of champagne before he ran out of pills and had to pour himself one more glass. It was very good champagne.

When the pills were all gone, Hecky stretched out on the bed. He sat up again, to take off his shoes, so he wouldn't get the coverlet dirty. Then he lay back and stared at the ceiling.

He was beginning to grow drowsy. He turned onto his side, drew his knees up, and stared at the bubbles still rising in the bottle of champagne. His eyelids began to flutter and finally closed.

Hecky's problems began to slip away.

Twenty-one

The funeral parlor was respectable, but small. Located in midtown, it had limited facilities for services, but then not many mourners were expected. Only the hearse and a single limousine were needed, since the immediate family would make up most of the cortege. There would be no long procession of cars crossing the Fifty-ninth Street Bridge into Queens, where Hecky Brown was to be buried, on a hillside of tombstones with a view of the skyscrapers of Manhattan.

The few mourners who did attend the service seemed distracted, on edge. They glanced nervously up and down the street before entering the funeral parlor.

Howard stood across the street, in the shadow of a doorway. He wanted to attend Hecky's funeral, but he was afraid. He had seen the two FBI agents sitting in a Ford coupe at the curb, writing down the names of mourners in their notebooks.

A cab pulled up and Florence stepped out. She wore a plain black dress and a scarf, and she held a handkerchief to her face. Howard could see that she was crying as she walked into the funeral parlor.

He wanted to rush across the street and join her. But he didn't.

Hating himself, he turned up the collar of his jacket and hurried away.

Florence came back to her apartment after the funeral. Totally exhausted, she had a stiff drink, undressed, and took a hot bath. Then she climbed into bed with a collection of Chekhov short stories, hoping escape from the nightmare of the present through fantasies of the past.

But she couldn't concentrate. She kept thinking of Hecky's suicide and of Howard's subpoena, which she had heard about at the funeral. No one, it seemed, was safe from the blacklist.

The doorbell rang. Florence's heart began to pound. She wasn't expecting anyone, and the sound of the bell was ominous. She got up, wrapped a robe around her, and went to the door.

She opened it slowly, leaving the safety chain in place. Howard stood in the corridor, peering in at her. His hair was uncombed and his tie undone. He looked unhappy.

"I've been subpoenaed," he told her.

"I heard."

"They want me to name names."

Florence shut the door and released the chain. This time she opened the door a little wider.

"That's what they want," she agreed, her arms folded across her stomach.

They looked at each other for a moment, then Howard said, "I'm not going to do it."

Florence was so relieved she felt like crying some

more. She stepped back into the apartment and Howard followed her slowly. He hesitated, then took her in his arms.

They made love for an hour. The tiny apartment insulated them from the outside world and the nightmare they were both experiencing.

Afterward, they clung to each other beneath the covers.

"I saw you at Hecky's funeral," Howard said.

"I didn't see you. I didn't see anyone, I was crying too much."

"I ran away," he admitted.

"Those bastards. What they do to people—scaring even you. But they can't scare away your talent; that's what's important." Florence raised herself up on her elbows. "You're a writer. Nothing they do can affect that."

"How would you feel if I wasn't a writer?"

"I know you," she said. "Whatever else you may have to do to survive, you'll find time to write."

"Suppose I tell you . . ." Howard knew the time had come. "That I'm not a writer?"

"I know you as a writer." She kissed him lightly on the tip of the nose. "I love you as a writer."

That was just what he was afraid of.

"I'm not a writer," he said.

"Howard, don't be defeatist." She sounded annoyed.

"Other people wrote the scripts, not me. I was only a front. They were blacklisted; I helped them out. My name, but their scripts."

Florence backed away from him. "That's a very bizarre statement."

"I am not a writer." There was no going back now. "I am a front. I front for blacklisted writers."

"You're not a writer?" She still couldn't believe it.

"I can't write a grocery list."

"You never wrote any of the scripts?"

"None." Howard was in pain. "Not one of them. I'm practically illiterate."

Florence remembered his reluctance to talk about his work, about literature. He always wanted to make love instead.

"You never wrote *anything?*"

She huddled against the bedstead, pale, her eyes wide.

"Don't get shell-shocked," Howard said. "I'm not confessing to a murder. Jesus, look at you . . ."

He got out of bed and started for the kitchen. "You got no color. I'll get you a drink."

"I don't want a drink."

Howard was afraid she would faint. "Put your head between your legs," he advised.

"Let me think."

Florence felt the world was disintegrating around her. Suddenly, self-conscious, she pulled her robe over her body.

"How could I tell you the truth?" he asked as he began to dress. "I was like a spy."

"Did you want to?"

"Of course, I wanted to. You think I liked lying to you. Lying is not my nature," he added, although it sounded less than convincing.

"I don't believe this is happening."

Howard was aware of a larger problem.

"Florence, I have to testify. Keep your mind on that."

"It's like I'm in bed with a stranger," she said, still in shock.

"So we got off on the wrong foot."

141

"The wrong *foot?*" She wanted to hit him.

"I was sworn to secrecy," he explained. "But we're both on the same side. Isn't that important?"

"Didn't you trust me?" Florence was beginning to feel hurt.

"I wasn't allowed."

"Did you think I'd lose interest in you?"

"You were in love with a writer," he said. "You weren't interested in me."

"Interested in you? I don't even know you!"

Angry now, she jerked the robe tighter around her.

"I shouldn't have said anything." Howard began to tie his shoes. "Now you're hysterical."

"Nobody's hysterical. When were you going to mention it? When we were ninety?"

"I mentioned it tonight."

"Because you're in trouble!"

"For a good reason!" he shouted back. "Who was I spying for? Hitler? I was helping blacklisted writers. Think of that for a minute."

Florence was unimpressed. "You lied to me. What are you really? A druggist?"

"Will you stop thinking about yourself all the time? You know, Florence, I hate to tell you this, but you know what you are? You're a snob."

"Go on," she taunted, "change the subject."

"You can't just fall in love with a person. Oh, no, that's not good enough for you. Catch you in bed with a druggist?" Howard rolled his eyes dramatically. "It's got to be a writer, an artist!"

"If you mean I wouldn't fall in love with just anyone . . ."

"What's wrong with a druggist?" A druggist was better than a cashier. "He's a person."

"I don't know any druggists." And she didn't want to know any.

"You don't know me, either. Boy, are you a familiar type. Girls who can only fall for a guy if he's some kind of big shot."

Florence was stunned. "That's not fair."

"Oh, your kind of big shot," Howard went on, "not just any kind. You wouldn't have looked twice at me if I wasn't a writer."

"Did you ever give me the chance?"

"I'm giving you now!"

"All right," Florence wanted to know, "who are you?"

There was a long pause. Then Howard said, "What?"

"I don't know who you are. All I know is who you're not. Who is Howard Prince?"

Howard couldn't make himself say that he had been a cashier and was still a bookie.

"You'll find out," he told her, "when I tell the Committee to go screw."

"You're going to tell them that?" Florence was skeptical. "That doesn't sound like you."

"In my own way," he hedged.

"That sounds like you."

Howard said defensively, "What can they do? Blacklist me? I'll get a front. He'll put his name on my scripts."

"You're not even a writer!"

Howard had almost forgotten. "So I'll go back to my old job."

"What was that?"

After another long pause, he said, "I ran a cash register."

Florence closed her eyes. "You'd go back to that, after all this?"

Howard began to quote Florence: "If the job's honest, and you can go home at the end of the day and face yourself. . . . So what if I hate it?"

Florence was touched. Howard was right: she was a snob—and he was in trouble.

She got up, walked over to him and took his hand.

"Howard," she said softly, "the Committee's dangerous."

He was grateful for her support. Suddenly, he felt braver.

"What have I got to lose?" he asked. "Hecky lost everything. Allie, my friend, he's losing blood. I'll get my old job back. What am I losing, some fake life?"

"You don't know what they'll do," Florence cautioned.

But Howard did know. "They'll take it all away from me. I won't be Howard Prince, the writer. I'll be Howard Prince, the cashier." He hugged Florence. "I'll still have you, won't I?"

She hugged him in return, then rested her head on his shoulder.

"Then what's so terrible," Howard said, "if that's the worst they can do to me?"

Twenty-two

Dark, heavy paneling covered the walls of the hearing room. Overhead lights glared down on the central arena —chairs and tables arranged for the Committee, the attorneys, and the witness. It was an executive session, but there were enough Congressmen, aides, attorneys, attorneys' assistants, recorders, and official observers in the room to give the session the atmosphere of a full-fledged trial.

Of course, it was not a trial, but everyone in the room—including Howard—knew the power of the Committee on Un-American Activities: careers ruined, witnesses cited for contempt if they claimed protection of the Fifth Amendment and didn't cooperate. Some had been imprisoned.

Howard knew this. But he did not plan to use the Fifth, and he didn't plan to cooperate. Howard had a plan.

The three ranking members of the Committee sat at a long table facing Howard and the lawyer from the network. The latter was rereading a statement he was

145

about to give to the Committee, his gold spectacles balanced on the tip of his nose. He ignored the noise around him, and he ignored Howard.

The Committee's counsel sat at a third table, flanked by two assistants. The counsel had dark, tousled hair and a pug nose. All three men wore gray suits that seemed too big for them; the counsel gripped his lapels and stared at Howard while waiting for the proceedings to begin.

The Congressmen on the Committee shuffled papers and adjusted their microphones. Two of them were not known to Howard, but the third—the chairman of the House Committee on Un-American Activities—was very familiar. A Representative from the South, he had snow-white hair and a heavy drawl with which he attacked government employees, teachers, entertainers, writers, and anyone else he suspected of sympathizing with the Reds. Howard had seen the chairman's angry face on television many times. The man could reduce the most hardened Communist to jelly during Committee hearings, or so the newspapers said.

The chairman banged his gavel on the table. Silence settled over the huge room as the chairman pronounced the Committee in session. Then he pointed the gavel at the network lawyer, who stood, cleared his throat, and began to read his statement. It had been written to ingratiate the network, and Howard, to the Committee.

Howard wanted to laugh at the hypocrisy of it all. He felt relaxed and confident. He could be as tricky as any of these people.

". . . and we would like to thank this Committee," the lawyer said, "for allowing Mr. Prince to appear and voice his approval of the great work you are doing for our country."

The Committee members all nodded together.

"Communist subversion is a real and present danger," the lawyer went on, "and you can rest assured that it will never be tolerated on the network that both Mr. Prince and I have the honor to represent. Thank you."

"Thank you, sir," drawled the chairman. "This Committee is here to help keep America just as pure as we can possibly make it."

Now everyone in the room was nodding—except Howard.

"Well," the lawyer told the chairman, "I can't think of anything more important, and I wish to commend this committee on the job they are doing."

"Thank you."

"Thank *you*."

The lawyer bowed and sat down.

The chairman motioned to the counsel.

That worthy consulted his array of papers and documents, then leaned across the table, his eyes still on Howard.

"Just a few questions, Mr. Prince. We know you're a busy man."

"Right," Howard agreed. "I'm busy. You know how it is."

"I have a few names here I'd like to ask you about." He held up a piece of paper. "Let's start with someone I'm sure you know." The counsel looked over his list, then said in a formal tone, "Do you know Alfred Miller?"

"Who?"

"Alfred Miller."

Howard smiled and asked, "Why?" Nobody was putting anything over on him.

The counsel seemed surprised by the question. "If you'd just tell the Committee . . ."

"Can't I know why?"

"You don't have to worry," the chairman drawled. "Mr. Prince, anyone comes up here and tells the truth, he's got nothing to worry about."

He pointed the gavel at the counsel again.

"Do you know Alfred Miller?" the counsel repeated.

"Which Alfred Miller?"

The network's lawyer shifted uneasily in his chair.

"Do you know more than one?" asked the counsel.

"Don't we all?" Howard joked. "Is Paris a city? Is the pope Catholic? Right?" He was enjoying himself. "See what I mean?"

The members of the Committee exchanged glances. The three men at the counsel's table conferred. Finally, the counsel asked, "Do you know Alfred Miller, the writer?"

"Know?" Howard considered the word. "What is 'know'? Can you really know a person? I grew up with Allie Miller, but do I know him? In the Biblical sense."

No one laughed.

The counsel said patiently, "Did he become a writer?"

"Allie Miller? He was a delivery boy. Fearless Dry Cleaners. I always thought he wanted to be a professional delivery boy. He studied it in college. This Allie Miller?"

"The writer."

"Which one is that?"

"I'm suggesting there is only one."

"Which one?"

Howard thought he had everyone confused, but the counsel talked on, undeterred. "Let's say the one you met with several times at Greenberg's Dairy Restaurant."

"Who said I did?" Howard demanded.

"Is it or is it not true?"

"I asked you first."

"Is it true?"

Howard was determined not to answer. "Who's accusing me?" he asked, looking around the room for the informer.

"If you would answer the question . . ."

"Which question?"

The network's lawyer looked curiously at Howard. What was he trying to do? It had all been fixed.

"You ask one question," Howard told the counsel, ignoring the lawyer at his side, "then you go right on to another question."

"Do you know Alfred Miller?"

The network's lawyer nodded encouragingly at Howard.

"You already asked that question," Howard pointed out.

The Committee members covered their microphones with their hands and put their heads together. They couldn't be sure if Howard was being evasive or was truly confused. A drone of speculative conversation filled the room. Finally, the chairman leaned forward to address the witness.

"Mr. Prince, the Committee was under the impression that you agreed to cooperate."

"That's what I'm here for," Howard said.

"We're simply investigating the Communist conspiracy in the entertainment world." The chairman sounded almost kindly.

"Are you saying I'm part of the Communist conspiracy?"

"No one has said that, Mr. Prince."

"A decorated veteran of World War Two?" Howard was insulted.

The three men at the counsel's table put their heads together, then the counsel said, "Our information is that you did not serve."

"Oh, of course. I was 4-F. How could I forget?" Howard shrugged. "I blocked the war out."

He was conforming to the stereotype of a writer. Writers were supposed to be eccentric.

The counsel pressed on. "Do you know Alfred Miller?"

Howard decided to change tactics. He would take the offensive and ask *them* questions.

"Do you know," he said, "that every week busloads of Communists are crossing the American border? What are we doing about that?"

"We are not concerned at this time . . ."

"Why aren't we? How can you justify such indifference? We should be arming to the teeth. Every young man should know how to use a gun. Why is military school only someplace to send you when you're bad?"

"Mr. Prince," the counsel asked with a trace of impatience, "are you refusing to answer?"

"Absolutely not. I'm at your service."

"Do you know Alfred Miller?"

Howard thought a moment. "How do you spell that?"

The counsel dropped his sheet of paper onto the table and turned to address the Committee. "Mr. Chairman, I suggest that the witness is deliberately obstructive."

"I resent that," Howard said.

"He refuses to answer . . ."

"I do not refuse. I just want to know what I'm answering."

The chairman summoned the counsel to his table. They conferred in whispers, glancing occasionally at Howard and at the network lawyer.

"What are you doing?" the lawyer demanded of Howard in a harsh whisper. "They can hold you in contempt."

"Only if I refuse to answer." Howard had it all figured out.

"Don't try to be smart. These people mean business."

"Relax, I'm handling it."

The counsel returned to his table, retrieving the list once more.

"If your memory is unclear about Alfred Miller," he began, "do you know any of these other people? William Phelps. Herbert Delany. Florence Barrett. Hershell Brownstein, also known as Hecky Brown . . ."

"He's dead." Howard wanted to say that he had been driven to his death.

"Do you know him?"

Howard didn't answer.

"Mr. Prince, you came here to cooperate, did you not?"

"A hundred percent," Howard lied.

"Do you think you are being cooperative?"

"I'm not lying."

"All right, Mr. Prince," the counsel sighed, "let me ask you another question."

"Feel free."

One of the counsel's assistants handed him another sheet of paper. He looked it over and asked, "Do you know a Patrick Callahan?"

"Who?" The name sounded familiar.

"The bartender at the Friendly Tavern where, I believe, you once worked as the night cashier."

Howard wondered how he knew about the Friendly Tavern.

"Oh," he said offhandedly. "Him."

"Do you know Daniel LaGattuta?"

"He sells fruit."

"You placed bets for Mr. Callahan and Mr. LaGattuta, did you not?"

"Well," Howard said nervously, "just as a friend."

"I remind you that placing bets is a crime."

"Howard," hissed the network lawyer, "is this true? You were a *bookmaker?*"

"Not professionally."

"My God!" The lawyer stood up and addressed the Committee. "May I have a word with my client?"

"The chair so permits."

The lawyer sat down and leaned toward Howard. He seemed to be having trouble breathing. "Why didn't you tell me?"

"What's so important? This is the Un-American Committee. Since when is bookmaking un-American?"

"It's illegal," the lawyer said, his voice breaking. "You can go to jail!"

"They were only little bets."

"It's still a felony. They turn the evidence over to the Justice Department and you're cooked."

Howard had never considered that possibility.

"They're bluffing," he said.

"You'd better hope so."

The lawyer got up and walked to the counsel's table. The counsel opened a manila folder, showing the network lawyer several documents.

"It's real, Howard," he said when he returned, his face ashen. "They've got affidavits, sworn statements, the works. But they don't really want to prosecute."

"See, I told you."

"They're willing to make a deal."

Howard knew what the deal was. "Give them names."

The lawyer nodded. "They're being very reasonable. You don't have to give more than one."

"Which one?"

"That's up to you."

The plan would never work now. Even if he was tricky enough not to be cited for contempt, they could still prosecute him for being a bookie. He had to cooperate—or else.

"They've got you over a barrel, Howard. You want to go to jail?"

Howard didn't want to go to jail, but he didn't want to cooperate, either. Florence, Alfred, and all the others were counting on him.

"What's one name?" the lawyer prompted. "If it bothers you, give them Hecky Brown."

"Hecky?"

"He's dead. What difference does it make? Let me see if he's acceptable."

The lawyer walked back to the counsel's table. They talked together in whispers and the lawyer returned with a smile on his face.

"Perfect," he said. "Dead or alive, they couldn't care less. A token, that's all they want. Something to show your cooperation."

Only the name of a dead friend stood between Howard and continued success.

"Is the witness ready to proceed?" asked the chairman.

"Ready, Mr. Chairman," said the network lawyer.

The counsel stood up again. "Mr. Prince, I ask you for the record, did you know Hershell Brownstein?"

Howard hesitated. He wanted to take care of Number One, but he remembered what Alfred had said. There was no middle ground here.

"Howard," the lawyer whispered, "you'll go to jail."

"Also known as Hecky Brown," the counsel prompted.

"Be practical, Howard."

"Do you know this man as either Brown or Brownstein?"

The Committee members, the counsel, the other lawyers, and all their respective aides leaned forward expectantly, waiting for Howard to reply.

"Either name will do, Mr. Prince," the chairman urged.

Still, Howard hesitated. He was either on the side of justice or of repression. But did he have the nerve to suffer the consequences? Was he ready to make the first real commitment of his life?

"Tell them," the lawyer ordered.

The counsel repeated, "Brown or Brownstein?"

"Just the name, son." The chairman's thick lips were almost touching the microphone.

Sweat ran down Howard's face as he struggled with his decision.

The counsel asked, "Are you refusing to answer?"

"Talk!" hissed the network lawyer.

Suddenly Howard was on his feet.

"I'm sorry," he said in a loud voice, addressing the entire assembly, "but I don't recognize this Committee's right to ask these kinds of questions."

There was a shocked silence. Howard quickly added, "And you can all go fuck yourselves."

The room filled with outraged voices. The network lawyer covered his face with his hands as the Committee counsel drove his fist down against the table, scattering papers, his face twisted with indignation and disbelief. The chairman blustered into the microphone, but words failed him. He swung the gavel, adding to the commotion and confusion. No one had ever defied the Committee quite this way before.

Howard fell back in his chair, as surprised as everyone else.

Twenty-three

Grand Central was crowded with commuters and weekend travelers headed out of the city, the lights above the platform illuminating figures hurrying toward the open door of the next train scheduled to leave. The stationmaster bawled the names of towns along the route, interrupted by blasts of steam that rose in clouds from the tracks.

Two men descended the stairs from the station to the platform, walking quickly and close together. One was a burly Federal marshal in a raincoat and a hat pulled down low on his forehead. The other man was Howard Prince. He carried his coat over his free arm, the other one being attached to the marshal's by a pair of bright steel handcuffs.

A conductor appeared in the open door of the train, motioning to the marshal. He wanted to get them aboard and seated before the rest of the passengers arrived. But Howard held back. He looked up and down the platform until he heard someone calling him.

It was Florence. She ran toward him, calling, waving, a big smile on her face. When she reached Howard, she threw her arms around his neck, and they embraced, ignoring the Federal marshal. He was forced to move closer to the two lovers, but he looked in the other direction, embarrassed by their intimacy.

Howard kissed Florence and said, "I'll make you a license plate with your initials."

"They don't do that where you're going," Florence told him, still smiling bravely. "I looked it up—they garden."

Howard was thankful for that. It was obviously a minimum-security institution—for political prisoners, he thought.

"I'll grow you a tomato," he said, lovingly touching her chin.

The marshal tugged on the handcuffs. "Let's go, kid."

"Howard . . ." Florence didn't know what to say, so she put her arms around him again and held on.

"Don't mourn for me, Florence," he said, smiling. "Organize."

Just then a small crowd came clambering down the stairs and onto the platform. People carried placards denouncing the House Committee on Un-American Activities. One sign read FREE HOWARD PRINCE. They all began to shout at the sight of Howard and Florence, and ran toward them, blocking the marshal's access to the train. They gathered round, congratulating and reassuring Howard.

He recognized several faces, Bill Phelps and Herb Delany were there, and they came forward to embrace him. He was surprised, and touched, to see tears in Delany's eyes—he had always seemed so tough before.

Howard's brother Meyer stepped up quickly to shake his hand, and then faded back into the shadows, where his wife waited. Neither of them wanted to be associated with the well-wishers, who were probably Commies or dupes. Meyer shook his head at the sight of Howard enjoying himself. "I knew he'd end up in jail someday," Meyer told his wife. "I knew it."

Howard recognized another figure hanging back from the crowd, his collar turned up as he glanced up and down the platform.

"Phil," Howard said, "you shouldn't have come. You'll get in trouble."

"Trouble!" Sussman laughed unhappily. "The rating's dropped fifteen points since you left."

He shook Howard's hand warmly. He leaned forward, whispering, "Howard, please, if you get a little time in there . . . one or two scripts?"

"But you can't use me." Howard was blacklisted.

"Can't you get a front?"

Howard laughed. "Why not?"

The Federal marshal led him toward the waiting train. Howard kissed Florence one more time and stepped aboard. He knew she would wait for him.

"God bless you, Howard," Sussman shouted. "God bless you!"

The crowd took up the cry. They waved their placards, and Howard waved back. He felt courageous, indomitable. This was the real Howard Prince.

The doors slid shut. The train released a final blast of steam and pulled slowly away from the platform.